MW01644937

Stories by
Stephen Carey Fox

The End of Illusion
The German, 'Mr. Kai' and The Devil
The Collector
Lou & Billy Joe
The Ghost of Yesterdays
Blame Jason Bourne
A Most Improbable Union
Everybody Knew ... Nobody Knew
The Elephant in the Room
The Robin Hood Solution

Artists, Thieves & Liars

Stephen Carey Fox

Artists, Thieves & Liars

Cover design: *Thief in Museum* courtesy of Shutterstock

Title art: Peter Paul Rubens, *The Holy Family* rescued from the Siegen art repository, currently in the Wallraf-Richartz Museum, Köln. (National Archives and Records Administration)

Author photo: chrisfoxdesign.com

ISBN: 979-8675799879

www.mickeysgod.info

Harbinger ...

'Yoo-hoo! Mister 'Stain'? Yoo-hoo! Mister 'Stain'?

The voice paused.

'You got a call down here, Mister,' she bellowed up the staircase. 'Make it snappy!'

Sarah Perkins, proprietor of the sole tourist home in Ennis, Montana, and Stijn (De Bruyne's) temporary abode, hadn't quite mastered the proper sequencing of first and last names, regardless of language or nationality.

'You comin' down here or not?' she bellowed up the staircase again. 'I can't afford you wastin' my money. The phone ain't included in your rent!'

Stijn De Bruyne had no desire to show disdain for Perkins, so, he trotted down the outside stairs of the tourist home—the only access to his room—and through the front door into the living room. Dressed in a print dress he suspected she hadn't changed in days, Sarah Perkins stood with her arms crossed under her bosom in a sure sign of displeasure and gave him a frosty stare.

Perkins, it seemed to Stijn, imparted an odd combination of someone who acted old (biting and intolerant) but looked much younger when she wasn't scowling. He wanted to react to the 'younger' Mrs. Perkins underneath, but she made that all but impossible.

'Phone's over there!' she barked, pointing to a small table next to a rocker with stained, flowery cushions. One glance told him the indentations corresponded to the contours of widow Perkins's ample backside. 'Make it quick, you hear?'

Stijn ignored the unpleasantness, the smelly chair and picked up the clunky black receiver.

'Hello?' he offered cautiously.

'Stijn De Bruyne?'

The voice at the other end was weak and tinny, as though spoken through a line stretched thin.

'Yes ... Who's calling?'

'An old friend … a friend from the old days in Utrecht.'

'Excuse me. Say that again. Who?'

'Thijs Verbrugge, but I go by another name, now. Don't you have an 'American' name De Bruyne? You're going to need one.'

Stijn recognized the all-too-familiar chuckle, full of menace.

'I don't know anyone by that name,' he lied, hoping it was a dream.

He glanced at Mrs. Perkins who returned an icy stare.

'You must have the wrong party.'

'Stijn De Bruyne, Linnaeuslaan 27, Utrecht?'

Stijn hesitated, starting to feel faint.

'What's this about?'

'You're not fooling anyone De Bruyne. You know me and I know you! So, let's cut the crap.'

Stijn, completely unnerved, hung up.

He started to leave the room when the phone rang again.

"t must be for me,' he said to Perkins who had moved toward him to make sure he replaced the receiver properly.

She retreated, reluctantly.

'Hello!' he said again, trying to sound irritated.

Stijn knew it was Verbrugge, the way he rolled his 'r's when pronouncing 'Bruyne.'

'Be at the Sinclair station on First and Grizzly in ten minutes, or do you prefer the authorities find out who you really are … or worse?'

Stijn slammed down the receiver, which startled the woman, and left it askew on one side of the cradle.

'You owe me twenty-five cents!' she demanded crossly, straightening the receiver ...

Cocoon (1985)

An Arizona Retirement Community in the 1990s …

Two residents pushed aside what remained of their lunch: cold, toasted-cheese sandwiches ('Wonder Bread'), small side dishes of coleslaw, and canned, syrupy—very syrupy—freestone peaches. Pushed all of it aside.

An outside observer might assume they did so because their food was unsavory or spoiled, or because they were ill-mannered.

No, everything about the place, the food and the other residents bored them. Perhaps they should have been more charitable in their thoughts about the others. But anything approaching excitement had eluded them lately. And both men had known excitement.

In a final act of defiance, or disgust, or boredom, and in near perfect, wordless, and spontaneous choreography, the pair of septuagenarians pitched their white-cloth napkins onto the table and, arms folded, leaned back in their chairs ... and waited … for something.

*

The place these men called home was a sun-baked expanse of park-model homes, palm trees, landscape rock and asphalt; one would be hard-pressed to find a blade of grass anywhere. Someone with a macabre sense of humor had dubbed the place, *Renaissance.* Considering the behavior of our two residents, a bystander might wonder about the suitability of that name.

Whether renaissance or dénouement represented an appropriate expectation for its residents, the staff worked hard to offer a warm, homey atmosphere to those in the autumn and winter of their years. The appearance of the dining commons, for example, which our disgruntled pair still preferred to meals in their own kitchens, was utterly charming.

Twenty circular tables, each with seating for eight, stood checkerboard-like throughout the room, each covered by a colorful tablecloth and those white cloth napkins. A coffee/tea bar sat at the far end of the room, which residents could use any time of the day or night. Directly opposite the entrance, about fifty feet away, was a panel of windows overlooking shuffleboard courts and, if you craned your neck, the hint of an enviable swimming pool.

Renaissance catered to a well-heeled, monolithic clientele. It would not be inaccurate to say it was 99.9 percent white. Excepting today's lunch, an anomaly, perhaps, the place offered all the first-class services and activities that well-off white seniors could desire, most of which were already quite familiar: comfy apartments, attractive landscaping, crafts, the previously mentioned huge pool and shuffleboard arena, bocce courts, dancing, and the entertainment world's biggest headliners, especially the greatly loved Wayne Newton!

Less reassuring, *Renaissance* included a secure (locked) wing, set aside for the demented when that time came, as it would for many. One suspects the propagandistic name, *Renaissance*, originated with the dementia wing, which the owner(s) applied to the larger enterprise to emphasize the positive.

*

One of the two men under observation had given up on his lunch even before he got to the sugary

peaches. He wore a wool tam-o'-shanter, its faded tartan clan unclear, which sat jauntily cocked to one side of his head, offering, perhaps, a clue to his personality.

In a momentary lapse of boredom, he turned away from his table partner to follow the gyrations of a curvy waitress sashaying about her duties. The young woman's low-cut dress, which, when she bent forward—deliberately, the tam-o'-shanter man thought—either to converse with the hard-of-hearing or set down a tray, revealed a fleshy promise.

It was not, in the view of female residents, a proper kit for a facility that catered, among others, most of them single females, to more than a few randy widowers. To prove the point, a mischievous smile, some might say a salacious one, crossed the tam-o'-shanter man's face as he strained, noticed or unnoticed—he cared not which—for a better look.

*

The second man was seldom without a sweat-stained San Francisco Giants baseball cap, a reminder of better days for his favorite team or, perhaps, of glorious days to come. His eyes didn't wander like those of the tam-o'-shanter man but stared ahead. Their irregular motion, however, showed the Giants man was thinking, but not of the enticing young woman whose head he was sure old men would never turn.

*

Neither the tam-o'-shanter nor the Giants man shaved regularly. Retired for years, grooming no longer seemed essential, not even in the presence of a cute waitress or an unaccompanied female resident, a widow, presumably, distantly seated alone at a table in front of the pool-side windows.

The two table partners had seen each other at earlier meals, of course, seating being optional, and at the pool, physical therapy, and shuffleboard courts, but they had never conversed. The Giants man didn't talk much. Depression? Maybe. Life at *Renaissance* had been oppressively dull for him since he lost Ruth, his wife of forty-odd years. Most of his buddies from the war were gone, too. Everyone interesting, except the tam-o'-shanter man and the woman across the room.

Something, recollections, and feelings past and present, would finally persuade him to end his silence.

*

The Giants man turned toward the rascally smile under the tam-o'-shanter. Time was running out, as periodic chest pains reminded him. He was certain he had a story that he should tell, a story plaguing him, churning to get out, a story he'd kept bottled up for years.

He's wasn't sure what to make of the story when he first heard it. It wasn't his tale or one with a moral he endorsed. Much of it was mystifying, much of it unsettling. Just maybe, he thought, as he sat across from the tam-o'-shanter man, if he told it to someone, the haunting would stop. Under no circumstance would he take this tale to the grave.

*

His determination to start a conversation with the man opposite came as a pleasant surprise to the Giants man. He had never been forward with strangers nor particularly talkative. But he began to think the horny tam-o'-shanter man was the right sort to approach with his unusual story.

The Giants man admired the man's uninhibited lust. Perhaps, because he would never have displayed such an urge so publicly, he was a bit in awe of someone who did, even jealous. At any rate, the man opposite seemed open to something new, as open to something to end the boredom as himself. So, the Giants man began without any pleasantries, as though the two of them were pals in the middle of a conversation.

"I met an unbelievable guy once," the Giants man said, clearing his throat, which was unaccustomed to speaking. He paused and looked across the table at the tam-o'-shanter man, gauging his reaction. There was none. Undeterred, he pressed on.

"Met him a long time ago, over coffee and pie, somewhere in Wyoming, as I recall. Name of … uh, lemme see … Wait, it'll come to me ..."

He was embarrassed at not being able to remember names when he needed to. They do come to him later, however, when they are no longer useful.

"What was it Bette Davis said about infirmities? 'Gettin' old ain't for sissies ...

"We were drinking coffee and eating pie at a café table, just a regular place, a swell place. I sensed this fella wanted to say something to me, but a couple of attractive women had his attention. Eventually, he gave up on the gals who paid him no mind, turned toward me and started talking."

Startled to hear the Giants man say something, the tam-o'-shanter man pulled away from his fantasies about the waitress, his unrequited flirtation abruptly ended.

"Huh?" he said at last, blinking his eyes as though to clear his mind. "You speakin' to me?" The brogue was unmistakable.

The tam-o'-shanter man's response, if you could call it that, made little impression, however, and the

Giants man pushed ahead. The tam-o'-shanter man returned to his fantasy.

"This fella I met pronounced his name like 'stain.' Don't ask me to spell it. Can't remember his last name, though. Sounded like 'brine,' but that wasn't it. You know, the stuff they cook our Thanksgiving turkeys in, out there in the kitchen. It'll come to me ...

"I figured him for a foreign dude. Had to be with a name like that. Told him my name … Dan Wiley."

The tam-o'-shanter man abruptly leaned forward and stretched out his hand.

"Archie McIntyre."

He just assumed 'Dan' was only introducing himself. He'd not paid attention anything else. The curvy waitress, of course.

"Pleased to meet you," he said with a smile.

Archie now seemed to have fully recovered from the shock of hearing from the usually silent stranger, and he leaned back in his chair again, refocused, relaxed, and ready to talk.

"Archie's short for Archibald, case you're wonderin.' You can call me 'Arch' if you want. That's what Doris did. Lost her about six months ago. Beautiful woman. Beautiful heart. Jeez, could she ever wear a bathin' suit!"

Dan Wiley barely acknowledged his companion's greeting and certainly not the mention of Doris in a bathing suit. Either Dan was afraid of losing his train of thought, or he was just not used to opening to strangers or he's too horny to think of Doris in a bathing suit. It wouldn't be fair to call Dan antisocial, but he wasn't yet ready to address the man across from him as 'Arch.'

"I want to tell you this fella Stijn's story … That's it! I remember. 'Stijn.' S-T-I-J-N. Like I started to say, I'll tell his story to you just as he told it to me, best as I can remember. When I've finished—might take a while—you'll have to decide what you think of it. Won't be easy, but I guarantee you'll find it as interesting and puzzling as I did. You game?"

"Sure. Why not? Don't feel like a nap anyway, unless you're going to bore me more than I am already."

He was careful to add a smile … a half smile.

2/

Girl with a Pearl Earring (2003)

"Stijn said he came from Holland, you know, but he called it 'The Netherlands.' I knew right away he was an odd duck. Interesting, though. He spoke with no accent. Perfect English ...

"This man was tall, easily over six feet. When you spend the better part of four hours with a fella you notice stuff, the small things: thin brown hair, hazel, or gray eyes—I've always had trouble telling the difference—and a long face with lots of creases. He was slender and broad-shouldered. He spoke with ease, soft and friendly-like. Made you want to listen to him. A charming man, really …

"Stijn was a painter. Never would have guessed it, looking him over. I guessed a banker or businessman of some sort. Said Holland … sorry, 'The Netherlands' … was famous for landscape artists and that's what he did. He rattled off some names, 'Van' this and 'Van' that. Never heard tell of any of 'em. Never knew any artists until that moment. Oh, well. I kept listening. Had to be polite to a foreigner ...

"He came West, he said, for the landscapes. Needed to decompress. Didn't say what from. I guessed something bad. Guess he thought landscapes'd relax his mind or make him famous, like all them old 'Vans ...'

"Shoot," I said to him, "the West ain't nothing but landscapes! I was damn sure of myself on that one ...

"But the next thing he said pulled me up short."

'Not quite,' he said, 'some are more special. I'm looking for those.'

"Smiled when he said it. Mysterious like. Wasn't being cocky, one of those know-it-all types, you know? He seemed at peace with himself ...

"Guess he thought I'd point him in the right direction, wherever that was. Heck, I'm just a regular fella with no great eye for those 'special' landscapes. But I decided to play along if that's what he intended. Silly, though. I reckoned there might even be some money in it for me, but it didn't turn out that way.

"Stijn told me if he didn't tell someone his story, it'd disappear forever. An important piece of history, gone, he said. That sounded egotistical. He'd have to prove it was *some* story to have played an unforgettable role in history ...

"Skeptical or not, it did get my attention. I figured Stijn was trying to tell me he'd be gone, too, along with his story. That's why I'm repeating it to you. I guess Stijn and I are both fatalistic. Big egos ...!

"Anyway, Stijn kept talking and I kept listening. Wouldn't you? When he'd stop for a sip of coffee or a bite of pie or donut, I'd say, 'Tell me your name again?'"

'Stijn De Bruyne,' he replied.

"See, Archie? I knew I'd remember it … eventually. I knew it sounded like 'brine,'" Dan Wiley added with more than a touch of self-satisfaction.

"He even spelled it for me. It's all coming back: 'D-E-B-R-U-Y-N-E. De Bruyne.'"

'Don't take this the wrong way, friend,' Stijn went on, 'but it means 'the brown one.' Ha! Not many of *them* in Holland these days!'

"Stijn seemed able to joke about himself, always an excellent quality, I believe."

*

Dan Wiley paused, pushed his chair away from the table and crossed his ankles. Head back, he sighed deeply, his mind being clearly and suddenly elsewhere.

A half minute later he spoke again.

"You in the 'Big One,' Archie?"

Archie suddenly came to life. Dan Wiley had found the key to rousing the tam-o'-shanter man.

"Oh, yeah. Came ashore at 'Juno' on the 6th with the 2nd Canadian Armored. We fought at Caen, seemed like forever, then advanced across France and Belgium and took part in operations in Holland and Germany supportin' the Canadian 1st and the British 2nd under Monty. You?'"

"Monty, huh?"

Dan barely stifled a wicked smile at the mention of George Patton's old nemesis. The American GIs in Europe held little regard for the British commander, but they worshipped 'Old Blood and Guts' Patton and his ivory handled .45s.

"Well," Dan went on, "we both saw some awful stuff. Me? U.S. 3rd Infantry, 'the Old Guard.' We were one of the few American divisions to fight the Axis on all fronts: North Africa, Sicily, Italy, France, Germany and Austria … 531 consecutive days in action. Rough. Not many guys finished what we'd started ...

"You know, when I was eighteen and enlisting, I couldn't wait to get my hands around Hitler's throat. By the time we got to Germany I didn't give a hoot about him. I just wanted to kill every goddamned German I could find. The stuff I'd seen ...

"This fellow, Stijn … claimed he did stuff none of us GIs could imagine. Seems he knew what we were fighting for. Him, too. Still, I don't know how I feel about the guy, the whole package. You'll see what I mean ...

"You're probably gonna get frustrated waiting for the end, but I'm not going to tell you how the story ends until it ends. I will warn you, though. Stijn De Bruyne was flawed. How badly? Hard to say. Ambiguous. Good bad man or bad good man? You'll have to decide. Game?"

Archie leaned forward for a moment, resting his forearms on the table, hands folded in front of him. He looked around the room. Abruptly, he pushed his chair back and stood.

"How can I refuse after such a fascinatin' introduction? First, though, let me see if I can't get some more coffee from that waitress over there," he said with a wink.

Dan Wiley nodded. A little-used smile crossed his face as he watched his new acquaintance move smoothly in on the curvy waitress. Dan supposed this was the man's practiced *modus operandum* when it came to women. Archie could have been twenty again, Dan thought. The Giant's man was a teensy bit jealous. Not too late for him to learn—and from the best!

3/

Out of the Past (1947)

The two veterans just introduced couldn't have been more different … or more alike. Born in 1922, one in a two-stoplight-town near Medicine Hat, Alberta, Canada—the stoplights would come later—and the other in Columbus, Nebraska, they had reached that time in life when people begin to take pride in how old they are rather than regretting it. Old in body but not in spirit, they would be the first to tell you; never more than eighteen in their minds, the year both became soldiers, went off to war and returned old men.

*

If Columbus, Nebraska, wasn't the geographic center of the United States it was darn close. Named after Columbus, Ohio, the town was a product both of transcontinental railroads and highways that spurred a burst of commercial construction and street paving in the mid-1920s when Dan was a boy.

The town of 10,000 was a classic, mid-size, Midwestern representative, its rooftops rising alongside grain silos from corn and wheat fields that for a time fed much of the world.

Dan Wiley's father owned and ran a hardware store, and Dan helped his father when he wasn't plowing, haying, picking or combining three miles out of town with his girl Ruth's father, Frank Dale.

The agricultural bubble created by demand during World War I couldn't last, however. Foreclosure and drought-induced crop failure eventually forced many farmers to give up, but Frank and his family managed to survive the downturn.

Dan was an average student in high school. Let us say average on the high side. He loved math but was never good at it, but he shined in history and geography. Dan followed events in Europe and the Pacific every night in his room, using a well-worn National Geographic map. Later, he would stand far above most Americans in knowing exactly where Pearl Harbor was, its purpose and why it mattered to the Japanese.

Dan didn't share the isolationist views of most Nebraskans. He knew something terrible was happening across the oceans. You might assume, even if you didn't know him, that Dan wanted to be part of it. His mother,

Betty, didn't want to think or speak of this possibility; she was worried sick for her son.

Mrs. Wiley had good reason for concern. Within a week of Pearl Harbor, Dan joined the army.

*

Dan and Ruth married after the bloody business in Europe was over and, in time, they inherited the hardware store and the farm.

Dan converted his father's hardware business into a farm implement operation that perfectly complemented local agriculture, including, of course, the farm Ruth inherited, which they leased. Patronized by other farmers who bought their tractors, pickers and combines from Dan, the couple helped to keep those grain elevators filled. Both the store and the farm paid handsome financial dividends, more than enough for them to afford *Renaissance* when that time came.

*

'Archibald Gilbert McIntyre.' The tam-o'-shanter man always shunned the given names his parents borrowed from distant relatives he never knew. Archie shortened his first to 'Gil' for a time but didn't think it suited his personality—nor did the girls who seemed ever-present—so he stuck with 'Archie' or 'Arch.' The girls approved.

Bow Island, Alberta, midway between Medicine Hat and Lethbridge, was a quiet town in the middle of a rich and diverse agricultural area specializing in beans—

especially beans—potatoes, sugar beets, dill and spearmint.

It was also ranch country, and Arch's family owned a small grass-fed spread of cattle that also helped, like Columbus, to feed a nation and the world.

Unlike Dan, Archie wasn't much of a student, but he could ride and rope with the best of local cowboys as soon as he was big enough to sit a horse. He was as comfortable sleeping on a bed of hay or a broken-down bunkhouse pallet as he was on a fine store-bought mattress.

Archie may not have known the world in an academic sense as Dan Wiley did, but Canada was involved in the fracas in Europe much sooner than America; Britain and the Commonwealth declared war on Germany in September 1939.

Archie, a dreamer like Dan who must adjust his sights, ventured, with no evidence whatever, that riding a tank would be much like riding a horse. This wasn't at all farfetched in the figurative sense. By the time Archie enlisted, tanks replaced the cavalry units of North America. He would need to learn to be as comfortable sleeping in a steel bucket-seat as on a bed of hay while dodging shells from the fearsome German 88 mm anti-aircraft weapon that his crafty enemy also used in an anti-tank role.

*

Archie McIntyre and Doris Burgess married a week after he returned intact from Europe in June 1945. A soldier needed a good woman to ease him past his memories of unspeakable things.

The McIntyre fortune that eventually allowed Archie and Doris access to a high-end place like *Renais-*

sance, continued to come from steak lovers the world over. Archie worked out an arrangement to provide *Renaissance* with beef from his spread, thriving under a productive lessee.

4/

The Unfaithful (1947)

"Stijn was born in Utrecht in 1922, the same year as you and me, Archie. His father, Cornelius, practiced general medicine at their home on Linnaeuslaan and his mother helped occasionally as his nurse. Her preparation came from a period of voluntary nursing on the Western Front during the first war ...

"After the war, she married her beau and settled down to start a family. The difficult birth of her son, however, left her unable to bear more children, so Greta De

Bruyne became a full-time art teacher at an Utrecht Gymnasium.”

*

‘That’s where I got my start, Dan,’ Stijn said. ‘I wasn’t clever enough in math and chemistry to follow in my father’s footsteps, but I could draw! Mother saw it when I was no more than five or six and she began to nurture my talent straightaway.’

*

Dokter Cornelius De Bruyne resigned himself comfortably to the reality that his son showed neither interest nor talent for medicine. He took both solace and pleasure in Stijn’s relationship with his mother.

When Greta wasn’t teaching or helping in the office, mother and son worked together on Stijn’s artistic education. She lifted his imagination and directed his strokes, tolerating his amateurish mistakes. Her criticism seemed harsh to Stijn. He was a child, he reminded her. As he grew older Greta became even less forgiving, an attitude she believed essential to his maturation as an artist.

Stijn possessed another talent—telling stories, which he loved to do and was quite adept at it. He read a lot, and that fed his imagination, a very fertile imagination! If he did something particularly bad, which happened occasionally, he made up stories to avoid a spanking. His mother called him her *verdomde weinig leugenaar* (f**king little liar). She wasn’t entirely wrong.

*

When the war started in 1939, Stijn was studying at the Rotterdam Academy of Fine Arts and Techniques. There, he awaited the inevitable military call-up.

"I'll just call it the Rotterdam academy from here on," Dan said.

Beyond brush strokes and mixing paints, he needed to learn the fundamentals of landscape painting.

First, a proper landscape doesn't include everything the artist sees, only the strongest elements; it's not a photograph. Also, a strong composition usually needs rearrangement of the elements or borrowing bits from different landscapes and combining them as a writer does with description and characterization.

Successful landscapes vary in the degree of detail—less in the background is best. A simpler background gives more 'authority' to the foreground. This difference in detail, just like the focus of light in the composition, draws the viewer's eye into the work.

Greens are critical to landscapes and there are many shades: Veronese, emerald, cadmium and so forth. Also, green has either a blue or yellow bias and the shade of green changes with the time of day. What seemed bluish green in the morning may well be yellowish green in the evening. With practice, proper mixing to achieve these subtleties becomes instinctive.

Finally, Stijn learned, the artist must not assume that because he's painted a landscape, he's finished with it. He must paint it repeatedly, in different lights, seasons and moods. Such a landscape won't be boring; instead, the viewer will see more of its complexity. The way a tree's shadow tracks differently through the day, for example and how harsh midday sunlight contrasts with that of sunrise and sunset.

*

Another aspiring artist, Natan Posner, also attended the Rotterdam academy, a daily commute from Utrecht. His father's family came from Byelorussia, one of the Soviet republics. He and Stijn weren't well acquainted, Stijn being a bachelor and Posner with a small family, but they got on well in the few studio classes they shared.

Stijn described Natan as a short, lean man, maybe five-nine and 135 pounds soaking wet, late twenties and already balding. He sculpted life-size figures in clay, then glazed and baked them in the studio kiln. Stijn admired his work very much and, feeling forward one day, asked why his figures had such oversized feet.

Natan laughed.

'That's so they can stand alone!'

Stijn felt foolish, but Natan touched his shoulder lightly and said he always got that question from viewers, even from prospective gallery curators and teachers.

'What can you get for one of those?' Stijn asked, pointing to the kneeling figure of a young man.

'It depends on the size. The one you're asking about could fetch between $500 and $1,000 on a good day. If I could afford to bronze it, double the price. Unfortunately, there aren't many good days!'

He laughed again.

Natan was kind. In exchange for Stijn's questions about his sculptures, Natan inquired which landscape artists Stijn admired. That took some thought; there were many.

'I know of Claude Monet and Meindert Hobbema, certainly,' he said, 'but I haven't studied them because I want to establish a style of my own. It's the same for J.M.W. Turner ...

'Perhaps one day a student will ask of an old man, '*Who's your favorite landscape artist?'* The old man, being wise but not humble, will reply, '*Why, I'm very partial to the De Bruyne school!'*

Both men had a good laugh over that one.

Natan once invited Stijn and two other studio colleagues to supper with his family in Utrecht, a most pleasant evening Stijn found. That happy time, plus the studio, made up the entirety of their acquaintance and social interaction.

Stijn had only a vague sense that Natan was Jewish—clearly, the family was not orthodox—which didn't seem particularly important to him until the deportations began in earnest.

The large-scale destruction of Rotterdam in 1940 ended their productive, learning days at the academy and drove Natan and Stijn back to Utrecht permanently. Because of his family, Natan never expected the army to press him into service. Stijn, otherwise qualified, avoided serving due to a heart murmur, a potentially fatal defect certified to by his father.

An overwhelmed Rotterdam medical staff called on Stijn's parents to help treat victims during the German bombing campaign. But the De Bruynes soon became victims themselves; both perished in one of the raids.

It was a shattering loss, but in time, being his mother's protégé, Stijn pulled himself together and landed a job teaching art at her old school.

5/

Soldier of Orange (1977)

"Okay, Archie. I've told you about Stijn, but there's another person who was central to this story. He represented the other side of the coin, so to speak. For him, we need more background information, so, bear with me."

*

"Thijs Verbrugge was born in the 1920s to middle class parents, deeply Dutch Reformed and profoundly nationalistic. His father, Joos, owned a *kruidenierswinkel* (grocery) and his mother, Beatrice, was secretary to an industrialist. Joos and Beatrice Verbrugge worked hard to achieve and keep their status. In the hyper-nationalism and unrest of the 1920s and 1930s, however, they grew increasingly fearful of those who did not overtly share their religious preference or nationalist fervor ...

"Beatrice saw firsthand the labor strife that threatened industrial capital and Joos resented Jews who refused to patronize his grocery, which he considered a model of its kind. Jews, of course, had their own stores, but Joos developed a ready rationale for that: they use their power to help their own kind, he told his young son. Jewish clannishness troubled Joos more than loss of their patronage. So, he taught his son that Jews kept to themselves—alien, subversive revolutionaries bent on undermining the moral and structural fiber of civilization ...

"If being 'alien' was not enough to cause Jewish expulsion from Dutch life, Joos Verbrugge also preached that they were Christ-killers and money-obsessed usurers, leaders of a financial cabal seeking world domination ...

"As the object of such an 'education,' Thijs must have been ready to explode with bitterness and resentment, even hatred. It is hard to imagine he could have become anything other than anti-Semitic ...

"Thijs carried Joos' hatred and his own pent-up frustration and youthful energy everywhere. Constantly attacked for his anti-Semitic outbursts by other students, he learned to defend himself, viciously, if necessary. Jews, whether students or not, became the principal objects of his rage. After school, Thijs Verbrugge took his rage to the streets where he evolved into a brutish street thug and petty criminal, stealing from Jewish shop owners, and assaulting those who challenged him ...

"So, Arch, here's the way I see it. When Nazism overwhelmed Germany in the 1930s and spread its ideological and violence-prone tentacles across Europe, Thijs Verbrugge became an instant convert. It is likely the other men attending the meeting on September 4 had backgrounds like Verbrugge's and comparable reasons for being present …

"Now, Stijn was obviously prepared to tell someone his story … I suppose the same way I was prepared to tell you … or anyone else …

"The reason I say that is because he got out three articles from *The New York Times* from after the war and passed them across the table to me. I kept 'em … He said I could … and I'll share 'em with you."

"I'll read 'em, Dan, but you keep 'em … for the next guy."

6/

His Girl Friday (1940)

The New York Times, July 2, 1948—

In 1931, supporters in Utrecht founded the *Nationaal-Socialistische Beweging in Nederland* or *NSB* (Dutch National Socialist Movement) in coincidence with other European nationalist, fascist and national socialist parties.

The NSB began in the classical fascist style, emphasizing the leadership principle. It sought a compliant government, fascist order, and state control. Anti-parliamentary and authoritarian it put the 'national interest' above the individual and social groups whose interests characterized Dutch society.

For a time, pragmatic leaders united the party based on strong organization and non-violent strategy: a democratic take-over of the country. The provincial elections of 1935, held in the background of the economic hardship of the Great Depression, saw the party gain 8 percent of the vote and two seats in the Senate.

But divisions within the party held on and in 1936 the faction supporting anti-Semitism won out. This led to a strong anti-fascist reaction from opposition parties, trade unions and churches that, in turn, caused NSB losses in parliament for the rest of the decade. After 1936, the NSB began to associate itself with the aggressive foreign policy of Italy and Germany.

The NSB demanded radical change: abolition of individual voting rights, corporatism, a duty to work and serve in the army, limits on the freedom of the press, laws against strikes. It demanded a reunification of the Netherlands with Flanders and French Flanders in a Greater Netherlands, which would also control a large colonial empire consisting of Belgian Congo, Dutch East Indies and perhaps South Africa. This state would be an independent, loyal ally to Germany.

The German occupation government, which took over the country in May 1940, forbade all parties, except for the NSB, which openly collaborated. Every new mayor appointed by the German occupation government was a member of the NSB. A month later the party's leader, Anton Mussert, called for the Netherlands to embrace the Germans and renounce the Dutch Monarchy, which fled to London.

*

The New York Times, July 3, 1948—
Following the German conquest of Western Europe in the spring of 1940, most Dutch people accommodated themselves to the occupation. Thousands of them like Thijs Verbrugge joined the NSB.

The Dutch administrative apparatus assisted the German occupiers in hunting down Jews. Their police rounded up families for extermination in Eastern Europe and trains staffed by Dutch employees transported Jews to camps in Holland, transit points to Auschwitz, Sobibor, and other extermination camps.

During the first year of the occupation, the government ordered Jews who had already registered with the state (as had Protestants and Catholics) to get a large 'J' stamped in their identity cards. In time, the Germans forced the entire populace to declare whether they had 'Jewish' roots and banned them from certain occupations and forms of public life.

Deportations to Westerbork concentration camp in Holland started in January 1942 and to Poland and Germany six months later. Ultimately, the government deported about 100,000 Jews from Westerbork to Auschwitz, Sobibor, Bergen-Belsen, and Theresienstadt and another 6,000 from other locations in Holland to concentration camps in Germany, Poland and Austria. Of those transported, only about 5,200 survived.

About 16,500 Jews managed to survive the war in Holland by hiding or hidden by people who cared. Another 7,000 to 8,000 survived by fleeing to countries like Spain, the United Kingdom and Switzerland or by being married to non-Jews.

Approximately 140,000 Dutch Jews lived in Holland in 1939. Only 35,000 remained in 1945.

*

The New York Times, July 5, 1948—

Dutch resistance to the German occupation developed slowly, but on February 25, 1941, the Communist Party of the Netherlands called for a general strike in response to the first Nazi raid on Amsterdam's Jewish population. The Germans cordoned off the old Jewish quarter in Amsterdam into a ghetto and, as retaliation for several violent incidents that followed, the Germans took 425 Jewish men hostage and deported them to extermination camps. Only two survived.

Many of those living in Amsterdam, regardless of their political affiliation, joined in a mass protest to the deportations. When the Germans fired on the strikers, killing and wounding over thirty, opposition to the occupation intensified.

This was the only such strike to occur in Nazi-occupied Europe, but the Dutch did not define it as 'resistance' or call the tens of thousands of strikers 'resistance.' The Dutch preferred to use the term *illegaliteit* (illegality) for activities that were simply illegal, contrary or undertaken without arms.

The Dutch, then, clung to a narrow definition of resistance. They did not categorize going into hiding as resistance because of its passive nature, but to help people in hiding they considered resistance.

Additionally, the Dutch did not consider non-cooperation with German rules, wishes or commands or German-condoned Dutch rules as resistance. They took the same approach to sabotage against companies that kept on working, public protests of individuals, political parties or newspapers and publication of illegal papers.

Covert resistance, which usually meant violent acts, initially took the form of small-scale, decentralized cells engaged in independent activities: small-scale sabotage (such as cutting phone lines, distributing anti-German leaflets, or tearing down posters). This changed as the war progressed.

*

Hiding and moving people—Jewish families, Resistance operatives, draft-age Dutchmen and Allied aircrews—were the most important forms of resistance in the Netherlands. Also, some Resistance groups, including one called *Utrechtse Kindercomité,* specialized in saving Jewish children. The number of those cared for by landlords, caregivers and rescuers totaled over 300,000.

By mid-1944 there were four major Resistance organizations in the country, largely but not entirely independent of each other.

Created in 1942, the 'National Organization for Help to People in Hiding' had its own illegal social services that paid a kind of dole to all families in need on a regular basis throughout the war, including the relatives of hideaways. In July 1944, authorities estimate the number of people cared for by the 'Help for People in Hiding' to be between 200,000 and 350,000 or one out of 40 inhabitants of the Netherlands.

The 'National Assault Group,' with about 750 members, conducted sabotage operations and occasional assassination, which made available many of the ration cards used by the 'Help to People in Hiding' organization.

The 'Council of Resistance' engaged in sabotage, assassinations, and the protection of people in hiding.

Finally, the 'Order of Service' prepared for the return of the exiled Dutch government.

*

When the Germans discovered those involved in the Resistance, they either jailed them, dispatched them to concentration camps or executed them straightaway. In total, the Germans killed 2,000 Resistance members.

7

Marked Woman (1937)

Stijn continued to tell his story to Dan Wiley in a bustling café that presented a sharp contrast to the slower pace of life outside.

Three waitresses moved smartly and efficiently from kitchen to table to booth—all of them occupied.

The owner, or a woman Stijn took to be the owner, an attractive brunette who acted as the *maître d,*' wore a smart gray suit over a white blouse. Hugging a stack of menus to her bosom, she went about her business, projecting both an air of pleasant command and an exquisite femininity.

Mediocre landscapes, most of them featuring national parks and each with a 'for sale' tag, dotted the walls of the café. They contrasted favorably with the half-dozen animal trophies, interspersed among the stuffed heads. The entire décor reeked of an absence of aesthetic sensibility.

The owner attracted Stijn's interest straightaway.

"Should I have been interested in her, which, being happily married, I wasn't," Dan interjected, deviating momentarily from his narrative, "I would've had to compete fiercely with Stijn for her affection ...

"Moreover, I sensed the Dutchman and the nattily dressed woman knew each other in a manner beyond the platonic. For instance, she made a point of taking care of our coffee while the waitresses served the other customers. When the hostess leaned across the table to pour, she made a not-so-subtle attempt to caress Stijn's shoulder with her breast. As she leaned in, he shifted his body and lifted his shoulder ever so slightly to encourage the contact. It made me both curious and uncomfortable."

*

"Suddenly, a blonde woman with a long, braided ponytail—perhaps as 'Heidi' might have looked—entered the café. She and Stijn exchanged momentary glances, as though they, too, knew each other but weren't quite sure of it ...

“I looked to see if the hostess noticed, but she hadn’t. The blonde took a seat in a booth on the other side of the service area before a large window.

*

Archie perused the articles that Dan showed him while the Giants man continued the story. Honestly, ‘perused’ was probably a better word for Archie’s reading than ‘digested,’ although ‘perused’ wasn’t meant to suggest anything other than Archie’s treatment of *any* reading material. It combined his ability to speed read and his disinterest.

Dan continued.

“Stijn sure has a way with women,” I thought, shaking my head in a way he wouldn’t notice.

“Do you know her?” I asked Stijn, referring to the blonde.

He hesitated. My question broke his concentration on the woman.

‘Uh, no … no. I don’t think so, but she reminds me of someone. But let me get back to my story,’ Stijn said, forgetting the two women and turning back to his companion.

*

‘It’s interesting, isn’t it, Dan?’ Stijn said to me pointedly after pausing, ‘how war asks things of people they never imagined themselves capable of?’

I nodded, seeing again the faces of those I killed, not all of them German and not all of them men. I recalled how religious I was then, with an unambiguous understanding of the Ten Commandments.

"I no longer kill, Archie, and neither am I religious … but back to the story."

Stijn saw I was elsewhere.

'You all right, Dan?'

'Yeah, yeah, sure. Just thinking about what you said about war.'

They stayed silent for close to a minute. Then Stijn spoke quietly.

'If you don't have to be somewhere soon and you have room for more coffee, I can continue with the rest of my story ...

Should we order some of that blueberry pie over there before I start?' Stijn asked, glancing again in the direction of the blonde woman whose booth was perpendicular to the glass pie cabinet.

"I began to think he was a serial flirt!" Dan said to Archie.

"This time, though, the blonde woman didn't return his look. I figured she was waiting for someone but not the man across from me."

8/

The Assault (1986)

A representative from *Utrechtse Kindercomité* contacted Stijn in early 1942. The organization considered him an intellectual, Stijn supposed, but he was never quite sure why they came to that conclusion. He guessed it related to his being an art student and teacher with left-leaning political views who would sympathize with their cause. He didn't have long to wait for confirmation.

The committee has a request, Stijn's guest said.

Stijn knew from the sound of the man's voice and his facial expression this wasn't a request. An alarming explanation followed.

As Stijn knew Natan Posner from the academy and because of some interaction with his family, would he consider sheltering (hiding) the Posner family should that become necessary? Stijn assumed the man meant 'necessary' because of the deportations. He wondered if Posner had suggested his name to someone in the Resistance; he certainly knew Stijn's political views.

The guest seemed to know disturbing details about Stijn and his family. Stijn's parents were dead, the man continued his explanation.

'You live alone in a mid-sized townhouse. You converted most of the space on the first floor, excepting two bedrooms, into a painting studio where he spent most of the daylight hours. The rear windows, floor to ceiling, open expansively to the sky with no buildings or trees to obstruct the light ...

'There, a landscape painter's dream stretches out before you, Stijn De Bruyne: rows of trees along canals and waterways laid out to protect people from the sea.'

Stijn, astonished, nodded, and the man continued.

'Your ground floor consists of a hall, parlor, dining room and kitchen; the basement a cold pantry—or root cellar—toilet and garage.'

Finally, Stijn's guest came directly to the point: Stijn's spacious attic. Clearly, the Resistance had surveilled Stijn and his house for some time.

Piet Schoepp, Stijn's visitor, asked if he could drop in one evening to confirm the attic's potential as a hiding place. Glancing over his shoulder while his guest jotted down some notes, Schoepp's extensive checklist of prospective hideaways and the power for good or evil it signified shocked Stijn.

He knew the reputation of the Resistance well enough to realize the request to use his attic wasn't a 'request.' Before Stijn could agree or refuse the request, however, he needed to consider his future should he refuse. He learned tolerance from his mother, and he thought the Resistance patriotic. But he knew it also carried a reputation for ruthlessness when it came to those who did not cooperate. If he acceded to Schoepp's request, would that make him a member of the Resistance? That certainly would put his life in jeopardy.

Stijn also remembered something Schoepp said during that first visit: 'Stijn, believe me, the Germans are going to lose this war and afterward there'll be a reckoning. You and I might not survive, but there is something we can do while we are still alive ...

'If, somehow, we do live to see liberation, people will want to know what we did to rid the Netherlands of this stain. I think you, like me, would not want it shown we did nothing.'

Schoepp, however, wasn't through. The Resistance made one more request: if he agreed to shelter the Posners, Stijn should also join the *NSB* to deflect suspicion he might be in the Resistance or, more to the point, hiding Jews.

His was an impossible situation or, as Americans would say, he was 'stuck between a rock and a hard place.' If Stijn decided not to cooperate with the Resistance, which revealed its hand to him, there was a strong possibility that one day people would discover his body in a canal. If he did join the *NSB* and later they discovered him sheltering Jews, he would wind up in that same canal! He also needed to consider what the Germans might do to him.

*

Stijn pondered Schoepp's proposition for several days. He had no family to support. He liked Posner and it seemed to him the Resistance was on the right side of history. He hated the Germans. So, he agreed to hide the Posners and assume a new identity with the *NSB*. Stijn figured that no matter which way he turned his chances of ending up dead were about the same. Would the *NSB* want to have anything to do with an art teacher? Most of the guys in the party struck him as ill-mannered—thuggish—and poorly educated.

A few essential questions crossed Stijn's mind as he considered presenting himself to the *NSB*. What if they investigated his background as carefully as had the Resistance? Would they discover he had a Jewish friend and harbored political views decidedly not those of their right-wing nationalism? Was he a good enough actor to pull it off? Was he brave enough? Posner had some responsibility for his family's safety, of course, but if Stijn didn't measure up, wasn't brave enough, wasn't a skillful enough actor … Well, there were plenty of those canals waiting for all of them, including Posner's children.

These questions and doubts haunted Stijn De Bruyne in 1942. He spent many sleepless nights but finally agreed to do as Schoepp asked.

*

'Obviously, you survived,' I said to Stijn, 'but what about the Posners?'

'Hold on, Dan!' Stijn said. 'I promise to tell you about them soon enough.'

9/

The Counterfeit Traitor (1962)

Schoepp approved Stijn's attic hideaway and the prospective host suggested the Posners move in before he contacted the *NSB*, otherwise there would be no point—deflect suspicion he belonged to the Resistance or was hiding Jews—to his application. Schoepp agreed. The pair also needed to be confident the Posners could make the adjustment and endure long-term physical and psychological stress.

Stijn undertook changes and additions to make the attic livable: furniture, particularly bedding; facilities for proper hygiene; and the food and water needed daily. He fabricated some minor alterations, such as blankets to cover the small dormer windows and insulation. Schoepp supervised all these arrangements and offered other ideas he gleaned from rescuers. It took the better part of two weeks to complete these renovations.

*

Schoepp learned the *NSB's* patrol schedule and decided a Wednesday night transfer to Stijn's attic offered the best chance for success. On discovering the empty Posner apartment, the Germans and the *NSB* roving deportation patrols would certainly conclude they were in hiding.

Schoepp picked his night. He and the family took a circuitous route through the city to throw off would-be pursuers. Mevrouw Leah Posner, the couple's two girls, Maartje and Klaartje and the oldest, a boy, Karel—a handsome family—arrived at Linnaeuslaan 27 without incident around 0200.

The group spent the hours before sunrise setting up strict rules for food delivery, for which Stijn would be responsible at first, behavior and the timing of other daily routines, such as emptying garbage and chamber pots. The children would be home-schooled. Since Stijn lived alone, noise from the attic would not be a significant problem. Keeping three active children cooped up day and night for the future worried the adults.

Fortunately, Schoepp had considerable experience with this problem. Still, it wasn't certain how much the children absorbed of his instructions and dire warnings. Any violation of the rules laid out by Schoepp would jeopardize everyone.

*

As the occupation regime recognized only the *NSB* party, it wasn't difficult for Stijn to make contact. A week or so after the Posners settled in and with considerable trepidation, he flashed his identity card at the soldiers guarding the entrance to Maliebaan 35 and continued up a flight of stairs to an open space with a large ornately carved desk. Behind it sat a somber little man in an ill-fitting dark uniform, devoid of identification save for the *NSB* symbol—a tiny metallic flag consisting of orange, white and blue horizontal stripes.

The man didn't look up, so Stijn cleared his throat and asked to speak to the person in charge.

'I'll never forget those eyes,' Stijn told me. 'Black and piercing behind wire-rimmed glasses. He seemed never to blink, as though drugged. ...

'Sit over there' the somber man said dryly, and without looking up he pointed to a single empty wooden chair among a group of people seated against a wall, not all of them men. Clearly, Stijn concluded, there was considerable interest in becoming an *NSB* spy.

'Fill out these papers while you wait,' the man added in an officious manner, doubtless routine in his case. 'It will be hours before someone can see you.'

He was right. Two and a half hours later Stijn finally met with Theo Vandermoelen, who introduced himself as the head of Utrecht's *NSB* branch. He was a powerfully built man and wore a black, tight-fitting, double-breasted pinstriped suit. His hairstyle and mustache were laughable imitations of the German *Führer*. Stijn stifled a snicker.

Vandermoelen's office was spare, not even an upholstered chair. A desk sat in the center of the room, a far less ornate one than the receptionist's, a couple of worn Persian rugs partially covered the old and pocked hardwood floor and, of course, the requisite portraits of Hitler and higher *NSB* officials hung from drably painted walls. There were no windows! Security, Stijn assumed.

Vandermoelen had examined Stijn's paperwork preliminarily, but he wanted to know more about the applicant's background and motivation.

Stijn had done extensive research ahead of time and did his best to convince Vandermoelen of his commitment to National Socialism. The entire interview, which struck Stijn as superficial—not that he wanted it to be more rigorous—left the impression the *NSB* wasn't especially curious about who they recruited. Stijn was relieved to have succeeded.

Stijn's host, who seemed to want to bring things to a quick conclusion, probably thinking of the waiting line outside, said Stijn would be looking for Jews. No surprise there. Vandermoelen shook Stijn's hand, snapped to a Hitler salute that Stijn managed to return limply despite having no practice and assigned the recruit to a neighborhood cell led by Thijs Verbrugge.

The principle *NSB* surveillance technique was to set up watching and listening posts, making note of those entering and leaving homes, any overheard conversation, movements inside the homes and in lights switched on and off. After the 2000 curfew they walked through neighborhoods, hid behind trees and, where suspicion existed, stormed inside those homes. Most homeowners appeared nonplussed at these intrusions, but occasionally some threatened to go to the authorities. That would have done them little good, as the 'authorities' were either German (Gestapo) or *NSB*!

*

In late 1942, a half-dozen men conversed quietly on the ground floor at Linnaeuslaan 27, a modest two-story brick house in Utrecht, home to the Natan Posner family and one other.

The leader and principal speaker at this assembly was Thijs Verbrugge. Others present were Peter De Coster, Joost Beeks, Martijn Baumann, Jeroen Pieters and the group's host, Stijn De Bruyne.

For the next two years Stijn tried to be the most incompetent Jew hunter imaginable. Each time the cell seemed ready to pounce he'd find some way to foul up the operation. Yes, it was a fine line to walk and more than once he was sure Thijs would be on to him.

The cell tried hard to succeed in its mission, but it proved even more incompetent than Stijn. Men of little education or imagination, they could never have envisaged that Stijn was precisely the sort of person they were seeking. Stijn thought irony was not their strong suit.

*

"Whoa, Dan," Archie interrupted. "Why are you tellin' me all this stuff about Stijn and Jews and his involvement with the *NSB*? Why did Stijn tell it to you?"

"Well, here's the only explanation I've come up with: he wanted to establish a positive image of himself, maybe to prepare me for a part of the story later that might not show him to be a particularly wholesome guy. But you'll have to decide for yourself about that. Just be patient. I promise you'll hear plenty of stuff about the guy to help you decide one way or the other."

10/

The Hiding Place (1975)

Stijn thought the Posners model hideaways. When the children frolicked, they tried to do it quietly. They studied and enjoyed parlor games on a schedule carefully and humanely set up and checked by their parents. Stijn soon learned that Karel became a formidable poker player, especially at his favorite, 'Texas Hold 'em.'

None of the discipline just described eased the Posner's minds of worry they might be discovered. The slightest noise at the wrong moment or a light left carelessly on might give them away. Fortunately, for more than a year the children's behavior never reached the point of alerting roving *NSB* patrols. Then, one night in

February 1944, security broke down and imperiled the ‘package’ in the attic.

*

Klaartje Posner became ill around 2000. Stijn was in his studio preparing for bed and trying to find the BBC’s clandestine Dutch station on his shortwave. The Germans employed directional antennas and listening devices to find points of illegal reception, so he had only minutes to get what he hoped would be information about the expected Allied assault on the continent.

Suddenly, he heard frantic knocking on the back of the false bookcase hiding the attic steps. Cautiously, he went to the bookcase.

‘Natan,’ he whispered, ‘what’s wrong?’

Stijn’s shaky voice gave away his anxiety.

‘Klaartje’s sick! Leah and I think she needs a doctor. What should we do?’

This was one of the threats to the family’s security they dreaded from the start.

‘Let me have a look. I learned some medicine from my father.’

Stijn slid the bookcase to the left, exposing the attic steps. He followed Natan up, both men hurriedly climbing two steps at a time.

Stijn found Klaartje pale and feverish with evidence she had vomited. Klaartje shivered on her mattress under several blankets, her pleading eyes staring up at Stijn. He felt her forehead and asked the child if she hurt anywhere.

‘Just my tummy.’

‘Where?’

‘Down here.’

Klaartje touched her abdomen.

'What did she eat tonight, Leah?'

'Just bread and some potato soup.'

Stijn was relieved.

'I don't think those could be the culprit, he said. Let's give her a …

'Wait! Shush! Someone's at the front door! Put out that light, Natan!'

11/

Madeline (1998)

Stijn scurried down the steps and Natan pulled the bookcase back into position after him. Stijn tried as best he could to calm himself on the way to the ground floor. Taking a deep breath, he opened the door.

Two members of the *NSB* stood before him, stomping their nearly frozen feet. He recognized the men straightaway. They belonged to an adjoining neighborhood cell.

'Stijn De Bruyne?'

'Yes?'

'We saw a light on your top floor. The blackout. What's going on up there?'

'Oh, that,' Stijn chuckled nervously. 'Nothing really. Relax, gentlemen. Maybe you know me? I'm also in the *NSB*. I can show you my party card if you wish. Anyway, aren't you a bit out of your district?' he said, hoping to distract them from more questions about the light. Neither man acknowledged the offer of the membership card.

'Yes, you're correct, but we were on our way home after the shift, not on patrol. We saw your light and thought we'd better check.'

'Okay, sure. I understand. Listen, the reason for the light is interesting. I have a telescope up there to help me learn the star constellations and to look at craters on the moon. It's so cold tonight the sky is clear and bright. Perfect conditions. Have you ever seen moon craters through a telescope, gentlemen? It ends the notion of a 'man in the moon!'

The pair stomping their cold feet on Stijn's threshold became curious. Stijn noticed the transformation and pressed ahead with his explanation in a manner intended to pique their interest further.

'Problem is,' he said, 'and that's the reason I was up there; the scope isn't working properly. I was trying to figure it out, cleaning the lenses, oiling gears, adjusting the azimuth … things like that. Okay? Still more work to do.'

The shivering men on the doorstep looked baffled. Poorly educated, they knew even less about the night sky than Stijn could have conceived.

'Yes, of course,' one of the men said. 'We understand. I've never seen the moon as you describe it. Perhaps when you get it working again, you'll invite me to have a look? Maybe I could bring my son as well?'

Stijn felt a sudden sense of relief sweeping through his body.

'Sure, sure. I'll certainly let you know. Your name?'

'Harald Bestaert. What is 'azimuth,' Meneer?'

Stijn relaxed further.

'It means the direction from here to a star, Harald, according to the compass. Like the North Star. We call it that because its direction from us here on earth is toward the north.'

He tried not to sound too condescending.

'Thanks for your interest and question. I look forward to explaining things to your son. I'll not forget to let you know when I have the telescope in working order again.'

'Wonderful! Goodnight, Meneer De Bruyne.'

Stijn closed the door and collapsed against it.

'Idiots!' he muttered to himself.

He rushed back to the bookcase and up to the attic.

'It's okay,' he reassured the anxious family. 'Just one of those roving patrols. They saw our light. I made up a story that put them at ease. How's Klaartje?'

'About the same. Do you think it could be appendicitis?'

'Perhaps. Have you tied pushing lightly on her abdomen and then releasing quickly?'

'Yes.'

'Did she show more discomfort when you released?'

'No.'

'What about her bowels. Has she emptied them today?'

‘Yes.’

‘That’s good. Do you have some Bayer in your medicine kit?’

‘I think so.’

‘Give her a Bayer, even two and see how she is in the morning. I think that and a good night’s sleep might fix everything.’

*

Stijn was right. Leah told him in the morning the fever broke and Klaartje was taking food again without distress. No more tummy ache. And thus ended their closest call during two fretful years.

*

“Stijn told me he never did fix his ‘scope,’ Archie. We had a good laugh over his clever deception and the gullibility of those *NSB* guys. It was a small triumph in a dangerous situation where the odds don’t favor you. I’ll bet you experienced plenty of those after you hit the beach at Normandy.”

The tam-o’-shanter man nodded his assent. His eyes suggested he was disappearing into a world of memories.

12/

A Bridge too Far (1977)

The fortunes of Stijn and his buddies in the *NSB* slipped precipitously when the Allies landed in June 1944. Still, the Germans were in no rush to cut and run, and until they did the *NSB* remained relatively safe from the Allies and from retribution.

After weeks of a slugfest in the nearly impregnable and deadly Norman hedgerows, the Americans finally broke out and headed east, presumably for Berlin.

Soon thereafter the British and Canadians finished pulverizing the city of Caen to root out stubborn pockets of Germans, which, unfortunately, was not the only result of their devastating bombardment. Together with the Second Armored Brigade and Archie McIntyre, the joint force advanced steadily north toward the Netherlands and its river barriers to the Fatherland. Field Marshal Sir Bernard Montgomery's ultimate prize? Berlin.

"Don't remind me of all that!" Archie exploded, shaking his head.

Following landings at the root of the Cotentin peninsula south of the breakouts at Caen and Saint-Lô, Lieutenant General George Patton's Third Army began to steamroll east across France from Avranches (*L'Audace! L'Audace!* as Patton would later say of his strategy), racing for Berlin dangerously ahead of his supply chain (as only Patton would).

The Red Army launched simultaneous counterattacks in support of the Allies. If all those moves had gone ahead as planned, which almost never happened in war, they would have enveloped the German armies in a giant pincer and ended the war.

In Utrecht, the *NSB* grew ever more nervous.

*

Nearly a year of bitter, deadly fighting remained. Stijn worried that if the *NSB* didn't kill him first, the Allies would eventually find his name on party lists, and he'd face Dutch and/or Allied justice—unless he could persuade them to believe his story of duplicity.

Could he count on the Resistance and the Posners to back him up? Perhaps not. What if the Germans or the *NSB* had killed Schoepp, found and deported the family?

Clearly, for Stijn De Bruyne those were intolerable outcomes. He decided he must find a way out of Holland and Europe once the Germans were gone. Even then it might be too late.

*

At the September 4 meeting of the *NSB* cell at Stijn's home on Linnaeuslaan, Verbrugge told them they would join a German pullout. No exceptions. They were to be ready on a moment's notice. The precise time depended on the Allied advance and the behavior of the Resistance. Although the Germans had kept the Resistance largely under control, Verbrugge warned its units would pounce on collaborators before the last of the Huns absconded. Traveling with the German forces would protect them from the Resistance, he explained.

Moreover, Vandermoelen explained to Verbrugge that Germany would need seasoned anti-Communist operatives to aid German resistance to the Soviets, he assumed, after capitulation. No one in the *NSB* thought the Allies would get to Berlin before the Red Army, but once the Allies arrived in the German capital, Vandermoelen said, these 'special' operatives, former Nazis with new loyalties, would work closely with Allied intelligence to undermine the Soviets.

"Archie, you can imagine Stijn's shock at this threat to his security and to Vandermoelen's grandiose plans. He hoped to get out of Europe. Now, however, he was to enter the heart of the beast to fight a new war! He must go into hiding. Where? How? Time was running out."

*

The following day, Tuesday, September 5, initiated what became known as *Dolle Dinsdag* (Mad Tuesday), the day the Dutch began to celebrate openly and *NSB* members feared for their lives. Either the celebrations would unleash the Resistance to go after them or liberation itself would be their death knell.

Within weeks, the Allies tried to advance into the north of the Netherlands and push on to Berlin by seizing key river bridges in the northeast part of the country. This operation, known as 'Market Garden,' failed and much of the northern Netherlands, including Utrecht, stayed in German hands. But for how long? It appeared the *NSB* could relax, at least for the time being.

*

As these events unfolded, Stijn remained at home, trying to figure out how to prevent his expulsion to Germany and avoid the Dutch celebrants in the streets. Under normal circumstances he'd have been out there with his compatriots, helping to pave the way for the Allies.

He began to consider he'd made a terrible mistake by taking in the Posners and joining the *NSB*. The family seemed to be doing fine despite their perilous existence and he didn't want to add his doubts to their worries. He made a conscious decision to help a Jewish family and must live with the consequences.

The Posners always needed food, which had become acutely scarce. Little did the Dutch know that worse was to come. Moreover, Piet Schoepp disappeared, his fate unknown. Stijn had to assume Piet fell into the hands of the Gestapo. Hence, he needed to develop a trustworthy relationship with others in the Resistance to guarantee his safety and the Posners' survival.

13/

Casablanca (1942)

A week after Verbrugge's September 4 ultimatum, a nighttime knock at his back door awakened Stijn. He grabbed his watch, squinting to see the time. He didn't dare turn on a light. It was 0342!

He managed to negotiate the stairs in the dark, fearing to turn on a light before he knew the identity of the visitor. He looked out a kitchen window, but it was too dark to see anything other than a faint silhouette.

Another knock! This time more insistent. Stijn needed to say something before he dared open the door.

'Who's there?' he whispered.

A woman answered.

'Monique Schoepp, Piet's sister. Please, may I come in?'

Piet never mentioned a sister, a Resistance precaution, no doubt. Should Stijn take a chance and open the door? Was she, too, in the Resistance? Perhaps not. She obviously knew who he was. Did she also know his secrets? These and other questions swirled in Stijn's head for several seconds before he came to a decision.

'All right, come in, *Juffrouw*.'

He couldn't see his visitor clearly in the dark, so he secured the blackout curtains against the kitchen's window frames before lighting any candles.

In the dim, flickering light Stijn saw what he believed to be a brunette, blue eyes, maybe, young, early twenties. She wore a deep brown, wool jacket buttoned at the front that draped far enough to obscure her shapely hips, black slacks and sailor's boots. Monique cut her hair short, he guessed, so she could it tuck under a cap. Her entire getup, plus her height and broad shoulders, suggested she could pass for a man.

'Please, sit and make yourself comfortable, *Juffrouw*. I'll make some coffee.'

Schoepp didn't hesitate to remove her cap and unbutton her jacket.

'Thank you for seeing me, *Meneer* De Bruyne. I'm here about my brother. My family is very worried. I confess that Piet and I were never close. I'm two years younger than him. You know how it is with brothers and sisters, always fighting? It's hardest on the younger sibling. Our family is close, so just because Piet and I didn't always get on doesn't mean I'm not worried about him.'

'Sorry, I don't have any siblings, but I can imagine what you say.'

'Thank you. This is difficult for me, *Meneer*, trusting a stranger who might not be who he says and could have me killed. I've got to believe you are not such a person.'

'You have nothing to worry about. Please tell me more.'

'Before his arrest … That's the last thing I knew what happened to Piet … he gave me your name and address but no other information. His instructions were to contact you only if something happened to him. We in the Resistance must take care. The first rule of survival is to give only necessary facts. The military calls it 'need to know' or 'compartmentalization.'

Stijn smiled at having already deduced that rule.

'It's enforced to protect everyone from exposure,' she continued, 'so I knew next to nothing of his activities.'

Monique was 'Resistance,' he realized. This fact alone relieved some of his anxiety about her arrival.

'I know nothing about his disappearance,' Stijn said. 'When was he arrested?'

'Three weeks ago!'

'Well, forgive me for saying so, but with him gone that long I'm not optimistic. The Gestapo is the Gestapo. We know their methods. They have unpleasant ways to get information. Then …'

His voice trailed off. Even in the dim light he could see that her eyes grew misty. Maybe Stijn went too far, he thought, but if she was Resistance, she must know the score.

'Sorry, Monique ... Uh, may I call you 'Monique'?'

'Yes, of course.'

'I'm sorry to have been so blunt, Monique, but I think we must consider the possibility that we'll never see Piet again. On the bright side, the Gestapo doesn't seem to suspect me thus far, so perhaps he is still alive and refuses to talk.'

'Yes, of course you're right. I'm trying to make the adjustment, put the best face on things, but it's not easy. May I call you Stijn?'

'Yes, of course,' he said with a wink, reminding her of her reply to the same question. 'I'm pleased to make your acquaintance, '*Juffrouw* Monique Schoepp'!'

The coffee was ready and Stijn managed to find a piece of gouda and some sliced bread and jam. It was 0400. Not too early for breakfast, he thought, quite pleased with himself over his ersatz hospitality. There were no sounds from above.

Then it dawned on Stijn that Monique might be his savior. He was afraid to ask directly for her help so soon, so he took a chance and decided to tell her about his predicament with the *NSB* and the Posners, then wait to see if she volunteered any help.

'Monique, do you know the Resistance helps to hide Jews?'

'Yes, of course. Why?'

He paused.

'There are Jews in my attic. A family of five. They've been here two years.'

'Oh, mijn God! They are here? Is that your connection with Piet?'

'Yes, they're upstairs. Piet selected the Posners because he knew that Natan—that's the husband—and I were students together at the Rotterdam art academy.'

'Aren't you worried the *NSB,* or the Gestapo, will get around to searching your home?'

'I was at first, yes. Then, at Piet's insistence, I joined the *NSB* to deflect suspicion. Who would imagine that an *NSB* member hides Jews?'

'I think it's possible for them to guess, *Meneer.*'

'Please, call me 'Stijn' …

'I know they could, but I have another problem. My cell leader says those under him must leave with the Germans, whenever that is—soon. No exceptions! I can't abandon the Posners. Who would feed them?'

'You're right, Stijn. You must stay here until it's safe. I can help if you want, but only at night. The Gestapo surely knows that Piet has a sister and if I'm seen coming and going from a strange house they're going to want to know why. That would put everyone here in danger.'

'Monique, when the time comes for me to get out with the others, I want you to stay away from here.'

'You're probably right, but I think you should come home with me tonight, so you know where I live in case you have to flee. Stay with me during the day tomorrow then return after dark. I'll hide you in my attic—like a Jew!'

They both laughed.

'Shush!' he reminded her, putting his forefinger to his lips, but neither of them could stop.

After a few moments, they quieted.

'You live alone, Monique? No family? No boyfriend?'

'No. Nobody. My family lives in a small tourist town further north. I never found a man that appealed to me. All too superficial and self-absorbed. You? No girlfriends? No family?'

'Same as you. Too shallow. My parents died in a Rotterdam bombing raid, so I have this place all to myself, with the recent exceptions.'

'What do you do, Stijn? What do you get by on?'

'My father was a physician and my mother a teacher. They left me enough money for my needs. I'm lucky. I paint. My studio is on the first floor, which I converted. Occasionally, I sell a landscape. My dream is to go to America one day and paint the West. Can you imagine how fantastic that would be?'

'America! That is a dream. I hope it comes true for you, Stijn. America seems impossible for me.'

He waited a few moments before continuing. She seemed ready to cry again.

'And you, Monique? What do you do?'

'I'm a nurse at the *Universitair Medisch Centrum Utrecht*, cardiothoracic surgery unit. My shift ended at midnight …

'Look, Stijn, we don't have much time before it starts to get light. Follow me to my apartment. It's on the *Leuvenplein*, near the medical center.'

'I'll be ready in ten minutes, he said, moving toward the stairs. I need to clean up and put away some things here as well.'

*

That winter Stijn came to know the apartment on *Leuvenplein* quite well. Two lonely people found each other in the middle of a terrible war. They gave little thought to the future. The present seemed all that mattered.

At first, they were friends, then lovers. It was Stijn's first experience with sex—and Monique's. There was plenty of fumbling around at first, insufficient foreplay … amateurish stuff. Eventually, they learned how to please each other and find solace away from the war, however temporary. Monique wisely cautioned that they needed to be careful. A pregnancy would have been selfish and irresponsible.

Stijn still had the Posners to look after and Monique her job at the medical center. On occasion, in the early morning hours while it was still dark, Monique came to Linnaeuslaan to help in the attic.

Even in the darkened space, while the children slept—they didn't dare resort to any light beyond a couple of small candles—the two rescuers grew close to Leah and Natan.

While the women looked after necessary housekeeping, Natan and Stijn indulged in unrealistic discussions of their futures as free artists; Natan struggled imagine how, when or where his career might resume. It was also true that Natan and Leah worried more about their children's future than their own. Nonetheless, both couples, if one considers Stijn and Monique a couple, seemed confident the war would end soon, and they would survive.

14/

The Getaway (1972)

The winter of 1944–1945 was extraordinarily harsh in Holland, according to Stijn. The Dutch remember it as the *hongerwinter,* and it led to widespread starvation, exhaustion, cold and disease. The Germans cut off all food and fuel shipments to the western provinces in response to a general railway strike ordered by the Dutch government-in-exile, which expected a total German collapse near the end of 1944. The government miscalculated.

Following the Allied advance from the Dutch-German border and their breach of the Rhein River in March 1945, the Canadian First Army liberated the eastern and northern parts of the Netherlands. They did not attack German forces around Utrecht, however, fearing massive civilian casualties; it's one of the most densely populated areas in the world. Their setbacks in the East and North caused the Germans to realize they were losing the war and they agreed to a truce that paved the way for an Allied food-relief effort.

German forces in the Netherlands surrendered in total on May 5. The Dutch then took the law into their own hands as happened in other liberated countries. Collaborators and Dutch women (*moffenmeiden*) who formed relationships with Germans suffered abuse and public humiliation. Still, many collaborators escaped Dutch retribution. Stijn smiled when he told me this, Dan added.

*

'Get up, De Bruyne! Now!'

Verbrugge stood over Stijn's bed like an angry schoolmaster. Was Stijn dreaming? He rubbed his eyes, not yet sufficiently awake to speak. As his senses returned, he saw Verbrugge rummaging through his clothes in the chifforobe. His first fully conscious thought was of the Posners in the attic.

'Pack only your essentials, he ordered, throwing stuff toward the bed. We must be on the trucks in thirty minutes. The Germans are surrendering, and we need to join them for our own protection.'

'Protection for how long?' Stijn wondered. 'If they fled with the Germans, Verbrugge's men might still be captured in Germany. Or they could remain in Utrecht and face justice there.'

Verbrugge chose the unknown, Germany, over the known, the Resistance.

Downstairs, Stijn grabbed some moldy cheese and a quarter-loaf of black bread that could have passed for a lump of coal.

He wondered again what the Posners thought of the ruckus. He talked to them about the possibility of his leaving suddenly if the Allies threatened German positions. They understood they would be on their own at that point.

The other cell members lurked outside the house, crouching or standing, casting furtive glances up and down the street, looking for any sign of the Resistance.

A handful of Germans, who either hadn't heard of the capitulation or chose to ignore it, set up an artillery battery a block away, inviting Allied shelling. It tickled Stijn to see the fear in the eyes of Verbrugge's gang. He wished Monique could share the moment.

Stijn needed to let her know what happened. How? He couldn't get away from Verbrugge. Then he realized she'd figure it out when she heard of the German withdrawal.

Stijn stuffed a few clothes and the food from the kitchen into a rucksack and the Verbrugge group was off on the dead run for German headquarters on the *Marnixlaan*. Beeks constantly looked for any sign of the Resistance. As they ran, gunfire, explosions and wailing sirens echoed across the city.

Stijn had learned to differentiate German and Allied weapons by their sound. What the gang heard as they fled was Allied gunfire, a realization that both frightened and elated Stijn.

*

Flying a white flag, Stijn's panic-stricken caravan careened into Germany from the Dutch city of Winterswijk. At once, the soldiers among them peeled off their uniforms and donned civilian livery from their rucksacks. They were prepared! Everything artfully arranged ahead of time.

It became obvious Near Münster that the officers and drivers planned to meld into the nearest displaced person's (DP) camp, the one near Mecklenbeck, four or five kilometers southwest of Münster.

*

'Dan, what they found in my camp,' Stijn explained, 'shocked me; I thought I'd seen everything there was to see in that war …

'The DPs needed repatriation to their home countries or a new country willing to accept them. This became a unique problem when it came to the Jews, who Stijn thought were about a quarter of the DPs in his camp.

'It's a horrible story, Dan. Most of the Jews had spent years in the worst of the concentration camps ...

'Eventually, President Truman learned that Army administrators had forced the Jews into DP camps with displaced Germans and Austrians, many of whom had been Nazi collaborators ...

'Many of the Jewish DPs had only their concentration camp clothes, and if not, the Americans made them put on *SS* uniforms! In sum, the Americans appeared to be treating the Jews as the Nazis had … except for extermination ...

'Those Jews,' Stijn said, 'continued to remain in camp for months after liberation, still behind barbed wire, still subsisting on inadequate amounts of food, and still suffering from shortages of clothing, medicine and supplies … malnutrition, depression and disease ...

'Fortunately for them, Truman did something. Despite considerable opposition in your Congress to allow intellectuals and Jews into the country, and a fear that war criminals might slip through, Truman signed legislation in 1948, allowing the immediate entry of 200,000 DPs. Same thing two years later ...

'The new law said DPs needed sponsors, and it tried to deal with the infiltration of war criminals and Nazi collaborators.'

"Then Stijn showed a sense of humor."

'If the United States had been serious about that infiltration, I wouldn't be here telling you this story!'

"We both had a good laugh."

'If we couldn't satisfy those restrictions, we faced being sent back to face prosecution or retribution. But, being creative, we 'non-repatriables' managed to find new homes in other countries, including the United States.'

"So, Stijn and the others sneaked in," Archie concluded in a tone that did not shy from disapproval.

"That's what Stijn implied, but he continued with a fuller explanation."

*

"Stijn said the surest way to get into the United States, despite one's background, was to obtain a visa."

'To do so we 'non-repatriables' needed to provide the IRO, the Counter Intelligence Corps (CIC) and the U.S. Displaced Persons Committee with proof that we were victims of Nazi oppression and never members of a 'movement hostile' to the United States. The DP Committe also required proof of sponsorship, a job and the sponsor's assurance the candidate was of good moral character ...

'My original sponsor,' Stijn told me, 'was an art professor at Cornell University in Ithaca, New York. Because I had no passport or other identity papers, I managed to convince investigators I was liberated from the Buchenwald concentration camp. My experience with the Posners taught me something about how to be 'Jewish' ...

'For the moment I became 'Benjamin Malik.' My inquisitors were far too busy processing applicants to discern or quibble over individual looks and ethnicity …

'Officials were overwhelmed with a mountain of paperwork, and they lacked support staff. So, like many others, I escaped careful scrutiny. I would get my wish to go to America after all!'

*

With his new identity established, Stijn sailed from Bremerhaven on a converted troop ship, arriving in the United States early in 1949. He needed only to register with the Immigration and Naturalization Service (INS) once a year. In the meantime, he worked closely with his sponsor in Ithaca.

A year later Stijn believed he had successfully evaded the restrictions designed to keep him permanently out of the United States. All the Nazi criminals and collaborationists who moved to the States were equally confident they succeeded in getting away with it.

Why? How? First, because regular police units weren't prepared to investigate these cases. Second, even the vaunted Federal Bureau of Investigation, as fine a national police force as could be found anywhere in the world, was not up to the task. Third, the job of tracking war criminals required unique qualities: language skills, historical skills and skill in researching foreign archives. Finally, and of most importance, investigators needed a sound understanding of what had actually happened in Nazi Europe.

In time, Stijn's original sponsor passed him along to other sponsors, even some who shared his passion for landscape painting. He dutifully reported these changes to the immigration authorities.

Free as a bird, Stijn De Bruyne headed west and began to use his Dutch name again. Not that he really cared about them, but from time to time he wondered how Verbrugge and the others had fared. He hadn't seen them since their days together in the Mecklenbeck camp.

*

"Are we about to get to the real action, Dan?" The voice oozed impatience.

"We're there, Arch. I'm sorry not to get to the 'main action,' as you put it, sooner. I thought you needed the background stuff to appreciate the whole of Stijn De Bruyne."

"Okay, okay. But how 'bout some more coffee and pie before you go on? A fella's gotta eat, you know."

"Excellent suggestion, but I have the sneaking suspicion you just wanna call that waitress over here as much or more than you want to eat!"

Archie shrugged sheepishly and waved at the young woman.

"What can I say?" the tam-o'-shanter man said with a wink.

15/

The Devil Thumbs a Ride (1947)

Stijn made his way across the United States, traveling by bus and hitchhiking when necessary until he reached Wyoming's stunning Wind River Valley. The contrast with war-torn Europe and the Mecklenbeck DP camp couldn't have been starker. After everything he had experienced, he could never have imagined a country so vibrant, free and wealthy as this one.

He took odd jobs in small towns along the way—dishwashing, bagging groceries, chopping firewood—just enough to pay for food and lodging. Ever the salesman, he let no opportunity slip by to promote his true vocation.

His benefactors (employers), he believed, would become potential buyers.

For food on the road, he carried a box of Ritz crackers, a jar of Skippy peanut butter and a knife. A grocery store manager for whom he had bagged gave him the knife, told him the combination was nutritious and would give him energy and taste good. Stijn quickly decided it did all three.

He came face to face with majestic red-rock formations in Wyoming's Wind River. Those and the canyon sheltering the river, offered Stijn a cornucopia of unique landscape material, just what he had been looking for. At the north end of the valley, below Togwotee Pass, sat the small town of DuBois. It all seemed ideal to this landscape painter, and he decided to stay.

*

The town's colorful location was striking and quite different from Grand Teton and Yellowstone national parks to the North. Most buildings and homes in DuBois were constructed of logs or roughly planed brown clapboard, many of them deliberately designed and built to disappear into the rust-colored environment.

DuBois began its existence as 'Never Sweat.' The founders tried to register that moniker (1901) with the postmaster-general in Washington—a man named Dubois—but he didn't find the name 'Never Sweat' proper and he decided to give the town an appellation of his choosing—his own! This irked the locals who insisted the town not be known as 'do-Bwa,' the choice of this eastern elitist with a French accent, but 'do-Boys.' Those cowboys believed they had something to teach easterners about democracy.

*

Stijn dined regularly at the Red Rock Café where he persuaded the owner to hire him as dishwasher in return for meals and enough extra to cover his rent at the town's only hotel. The café had obviously hit hard times; the attractive owner, Marge Balfour, performed triple-duty as owner, cook, and waitress.

'I'm doing the best I can,' she confided to Stijn only days after his arrival. They had begun to talk while he ate or worked in the kitchen and had taken note of his ill-disguised interest in her if he were really trying to hide it. Naturally, she was curious to know why this worldly man—it didn't take her long to figure that out—had decided to hang around a small, nondescript western town.

Taking measure of the precariousness of the Red Rock Café and the allure of Marge Balfour, Stijn had struggled since setting foot in the Red Rock Café to come up with a solution or solutions to her financial hardship. Balfour was quickly becoming Stijn's principal interest in DuBois … beyond his painting, of course.

'I have a handful of reliable customers,' she sighed, dropping heavily into a seat at his table one rainy morning, 'but as things stand, I can't keep up, physically or financially. You must have seen that. Doing this alone I just don't have the energy, and I certainly can't keep up with the bills!'

Stijn nodded his appreciation of Marge's predicament and growing despair and took another sip of coffee. Had she known him better at that early stage of their relationship, she would have seen it in his eyes that he was close to finding a way out.

*

Marge came of age in a small Midwestern town, the kind of place where everybody knows everybody and their business. Her father worked at the post office and her mother took in washing and ironing for wealthier townspeople. It would not be farfetched to say that the family's economic situation met the definition of 'hardscrabble.'

Marge, an only child, showed a streak of independence from an early age. She frequently demonstrated that she had a mind of her own, independent of the crowd and the usual behavior of teenagers who, in general, found comfort in conformity. Put another way, Marge Balfour was okay without a coterie of friends to hang out with and from whom to take direction.

Leaving that small town became a driving force in her life. She couldn't wait to strike out on her own and discover what the world offered. She found that drive through contact with strangers from out of town, the kind of people who could tell her of that world. Those encounters, so vital to Marge's growing wanderlust, could only happen in the town's only restaurant. So, as soon as the law allowed, she began, at fifteen, to wait tables.

Marge's instinct proved correct. From strangers passing through town she heard exciting stories, mostly about the West where, according to more than a few customers whose fevered and figurative imaginations, gold itched to be taken .

Surprisingly, they spoke not of California but of the wide-open space of the country encompassed by the North and South tributaries of the Platte River, Nebraska's longest and most important. Both tributaries arose from snowmelt in the eastern Rockies east of the Continental Divide in Colorado. It's called the Rabbit Ears Range, not far from Grizzly Creek and Little Grizzly Creek in northern Colorado high country and once the home of the grizzly bear and gray wolf.

The notion of 'gold' in 'them hills,' as Marge's customers put it, was hardly a unique western fable, but it stirred Marge's imagination and evolving wanderlust.

Marge, an incurable romantic and a woman looking for the main chance, couldn't wait to leave that small town. It wasn't that she had something against such towns as hers. No, she simply wanted to see something more of the world, large or small.

She tried college in an adjoining state, but academics bored her (too theoretical) as much or more than the pace of life her small town. One aspect of the state university, however, was anything but humdrum: the senior star football player, a.k.a. the BMOC, 'Big Man on Campus.'

*

Jack Balfour, the BMOC in question, hailed from Montana. Townspeople in Bozeman remembered that he'd always had an eye for the girls, a roving eye. Having that roving eye, those townspeople said, started in Jack's during transition from boyhood to puberty, and only increased with time.

Jack spotted Marge the moment she lighted on campus. He lived at the Phi Delta Theta fraternity house, but the university confined Marge to a curfew-restrictive dorm with the rest of the freshman girls, the practice in those days.

Jack, who grew up on a ranch, the kind of place Marge dreamed of as she waited those tables in that dreary 'hardscrabble' town of hers. She learned he could ride, rope and brand; Marge was eager to get out of the dorm and roped and branded.

They managed through pure luck and the little biology Marge absorbed in high school to carry out an energetic sex life and make sure Marge was back in her dorm every night before curfew without her becoming pregnant.

When Jack graduated and announced he was returning to Montana, he proposed. The eager, love-smitten Marge, more than ready to move on, never hesitated. 'Yes!' was her resounding reply. Moving on, however did not include marriage.

With seed money from Jack's father, they started a small ranch near Miles City, in the flatter, eastern part of the state. It worked to their satisfaction for a time, but Jack longed for the mountains to the West. He was never a careful student of economics at State. Being the star football player and BMOC, he never felt the need.

Now there was need. The hardworking couple just couldn't make their ranch sustainable. They put what extra money they could into it, but it bought them no future.

Foreclosure beckoned after a few lean years of procrastination. There was a small amount of capital left, just enough for a down payment on a small café in Dubois, just the kind of situation, Marge argued, to give them a fresh start. Reluctantly, Jack agreed; he had no solution for the failing ranch. So, they packed up and moved to Wyoming.

*

The couple's fresh start, which lasted only briefly, included fertility testing to determine the reason for Marge's inability to conceive. Marge's inability? The fault lay with Jack Balfour: he was sterile. Soon, Jack, unbalanced and unable to cope with multiple failures, particularly the one related to procreation—a crushing blow to a BMOC—took to drink and ran off with the Red Rock Café's waitress.

Janet Phillips, the lady in question, was a buxom flirt who reminded him of the good old days, including, he imagined, his gridiron heroics. Unfortunately, Jack's new 'friend' neither knew of, nor cared for any of that. Simply put, Janet thought Jack a cute and funny meal ticket. Nothing more.

In quick order the runaways incurred large drinking and gambling bills in Las Vegas and Reno, which Jack charged against the café's mortgage. As Marge was a cosigner, Jack's spending spree left her with sole responsibility for his debts.

It wasn't known with certainty what became of Jack. There were rumors of his excessive drinking; some had it, without confirmation, that four years after he fled

DuBois with Janet, some kids found him in a seedy alley in Austin, Nevada, suffocated by his own vomit. The promise of gold that Marge had heard about so often in that Midwest restaurant had never 'panned out' for Jack Balfour.

16/

Larceny, Inc. (1942)

Stijn spoke often to Marge of his passion for landscape art and his love for the work of landscape specialists Claude Monet, George Caleb Bingham, Frederic Remington, Frederic Edwin Church, Winslow Homer and George Catlin. Art books were his constant companions, and he never much minded the heft they added to his suitcase. From them, he showered Marge with nuanced dissertations on the techniques of the masters. She, in turn, bore his passion gallantly and tirelessly.

'I have a proposition for you, Marge,' Stijn offered after a few weeks, 'and I hope you'll consider it. Might be the salvation for both of us. Interested?

‘I might be, after you tell me what it is!’ she said with a laugh, affectionately punching his shoulder.

‘Okay! Okay! Take it easy!’ He put his head back and laughed with her.

‘Let me mount a few select pieces of my work on your walls. If you can do without some of those stuffed animal heads and beer signs that net you nothing, we can sell a few landscapes, drum up more café clientele and share the profits … let’s say, 60/40 in your favor.’

She looked interested, so, he continued his pitch.

‘This valley and the parks to the North bring thousands of tourists through DuBois. There seem to be few alternative roads for getting across the state. I’m sure we could relieve those travelers of some of their hard-earned cash. There might even be some interest from local ranchers who did well during and after the war.’

‘What could we expect to get for one of your pieces?’ Marge said. ‘I haven’t the faintest idea of the art market.’

‘Oh, anywhere from $100 to $250, dependent largely on the size.’

Marge hesitated only briefly. Then a smile crossed her face.

‘Stijn De Bruyne,’ she exclaimed, ‘you’re on! Let’s shake on it.’

When she extended her hand, he grasped it and, without having given it much thought beforehand, pulled her toward him and kissed her cheek. That was all the encouragement Marge Balfour needed. She slumped into his arms and looked up longingly. Their lips touched tenderly. Stijn realized hadn’t felt this way about a woman since

Monique Schoepp. After supper, he moved from the hotel into Marge's apartment.

They lived happily for close to a year. Stijn found that traveling, conversation, cooking together and love-making with a mature woman produced an unanticipated level of satisfaction.

*

Eventually, Stijn's landscapes proved a godsend. Word spread of the DuBois 'gallery,' its featured artist, and its attractive patron. Tourists poured into the Red Rock Café, which gave Marge a good start on her debts. She hired two waitresses and a dishwasher. Stijn loved watching her swish around the tables in her new role as owner/hostess.

While a trusted waitress occasionally held the reins of the café, Stijn and Marge made several outings to the Tetons and Yellowstone. Tourists seemed never to tire of Stijn's treatment of those unique, frightening examples of geologic anger and he tried to keep his perspectives fresh to attract new clients and bring back established ones.

Gradually, however, it became clear to both people that new landscapes of one kind and another beckoned Stijn. He returned to Montana for a weekend alone. Marge stayed behind as it was a holiday weekend.

*

Stijn spent an afternoon in July doing what he loved. His rejuvenated brushes told another story of the Madison River and the range of the same name, whose shoulders sheltered the meandering stream. This canvas would be for Marge, he vowed, not some well-heeled stranger.

It proved a long hike up the hill overlooking Ennis. On the other side lay Virginia City. While the sun lasted, it bounced heat off the white, concrete road, baking and blinding him as he trudged on with easel, paints, and brushes. Long and strenuous, yes, but the mountain vista and river that lay before him was well worth the effort.

An hour after he had set up his easel and began to work, a sudden squall came up, gusting upriver toward him. The sudden, stabbing wind tumbled his hat across the hardscrabble and onto the Old Virginia City highway. He didn't care. He closed his eyes and felt the wind play with his hair like a masseuse with a thousand tantalizing fingers.

Far below, a handful of fishermen in small boats struggled in the powerful wind to reel in their lines and find shelter. The roiling black clouds above and whitecaps that pushed against the steel-gray river offered Stijn an extraordinary portrait of raw nature. The swirling gusts caused the long sea-green grasses on the riverbank and fields beyond to undulate in a gentle rhythm as though part of a Hawaiian hula.

He gave little heed to the cool wind and rain that began to pelt him. He rigged a tent with his shirt, putting the tail over his easel and the collar over his head to protect what he had already accomplished. His brushes moved swiftly to capture as much of the scene as he remembered it before the rain collapsed his shirt-tent and ruined his work. Unlike the harried fishermen, the artist had become one with the storm, enjoying a unique sense of ethereal tranquility amid the maelstrom.

17/

The Final Heist (1991)

Following some weeks of restlessness and discussion, the decision that both of them knew could not be put off any longer arrived. It came on a memorable October afternoon just after a magnificent mountain squall.

*

In sharp contrast to trunks of mostly white bark splotched with black, the golden leaves of the quaking aspens glistened and fluttered in their glorious fall regalia. Through the leaves the sun, acting out its essential role in nature's drama, squinted warmly then coolly between dark and light clouds that scuttled smartly along in the wind.

The two of them sat on a bench in front of the Red Rock Café. Stijn put his arm around Marge and promised he'd call often and occasionally send a landscape or two to keep up a healthy tourist flow.

Then he pulled slightly away, relaxing the contact between them. She sensed the physical change and accompanying mood and asked what was wrong.

'Marge, honey,' he began slowly, 'we've been all over this before, but I want the reason for my leaving to be clear. You've got the café to look after. It's your life! You can't keep hiring somebody to run the place while you're traveling with me, and I've run out of fresh landscapes; that's why I must go up into Montana. But I want you to know how devastating it is for me to realize that my finding new inspiration means leaving you, even for a minute.'

Then he turned mysterious.

'There's also that other idea for our future I've been mulling over, the one I've mentioned occasionally. I may have to go back east to discover what would be involved to make it work. At any rate, if Montana or the New York thing pans out … maybe both will … I'll come back to you richer and more in love than ever.'

'Stijn De Bruyne, I swear you're the biggest bullshitter west of the Pecos!'

They laughed loudly.

'Tell me about that New York dream of yours, Stijn. Humor me.'

Stijn, who was sure how serious his lover was, nonetheless went over the New York plan that'd been churning inside him for months. Marge, if she agreed, would play a small but critical role; it had the possibility of enriching them both.

'I don't have all the details worked out yet,' he admitted. 'It's still pretty sketchy, so I'll be gone for several months. First Montana, then New York … possibly. Before I leave, I need to know you believe in me and trust me. Can you trust me with the plan, Marge? Sketchy as it is? If you say no, I won't go beyond Montana.'

She hesitated, trying to sort through what trusting Stijn De Bruyne might entail, confused about the mysterious New York thing and especially her role in it, not happy about his leaving but not prepared to stop him. So, after a few moments she put her arm through his, leaned her head on his shoulder and squeezed tightly against him.

'Yes, of course I trust you. I'd never try to prevent your fulfilling your dreams,' she said despite her tears.

She knew that her commitment wasn't entirely without reservation; he sensed it as well, but it was time.

*

Dressed warmly in mackinaws against the chilly, fall breeze Stijn and Marge stood and then walked quietly toward the bus stop.

He took her into his arms again as the bus from Riverton pulled to a stop, kissing her tenderly and softly brushing away a tear with the back of his fingers on his right hand. Then, as the local with Stijn aboard headed north down Main in the direction of the Togwotee, Marge walked onto the street, trailing the bus for a few feet as though she wanted to be close to him until she couldn't.

18/

When a Stranger Calls (1979)

'Yoo-hoo! Mister 'Stain'? Yoo-hoo! Mister 'Stain'? You got a call down here, Mister,' his landlady bellowed up the staircase. 'Make it snappy!'

Sarah Perkins, proprietor of the sole tourist home in Ennis, Montana, Stijn's temporary abode, hadn't quite mastered the proper sequencing of first and last names, regardless of language or nationality.

'You comin' down here?' she bellowed up the staircase again. 'I can't afford you wasting my money. The phone ain't included in your rent!'

Stijn De Bruyne had no desire to show disdain for Perkins, so, he trotted down the outside stairs of the tourist home—the only access to his room—and through the front door into the living room. Dressed in a print dress he suspected she hadn't changed in days, Sarah Perkins stood with her arms crossed under her bosom in a sure sign of displeasure and gave him a frosty stare.

Perkins, it seemed to Stijn, imparted an odd combination of someone who acted old (biting and intolerant) but looked much younger when she wasn't scowling. He wanted to react to the 'younger' Mrs. Perkins underneath, but she made that all but impossible.

'Phone's over there!' she barked, pointing to a small table next to a rocker with stained, flowery cushions. One glance told him the indentations corresponded to the contours of widow Perkins's ample backside. 'Make it quick, you hear?'

Stijn ignored the unpleasantness, the smelly chair and picked up the clunky black receiver.

'Hello?' he said cautiously.

'Stijn De Bruyne?'

The voice at the other end was weak and tinny, as though spoken through a thinly stretched line.

'Yes ... Who's calling?'

'An old friend … a friend from the old days in Utrecht.'

'Excuse me. Say that again. Who?'

'Thijs Verbrugge, but I go by another name. Don't you have an 'American' name De Bruyne? You're going to need one.'

Stijn recognized the all-too-familiar chuckle, full of menace.

'I don't know anyone by that name,' he lied, hoping it was a dream. 'You must have the wrong party.'

'Stijn De Bruyne, Linnaeuslaan 27, Utrecht?'

Stijn hesitated, starting to feel faint.

'What's this all about?'

'You're not fooling anyone De Bruyne. You know me and I know you! So, let's cut the crap.'

Stijn, completely unnerved, hung up.

He started to leave the room when the phone rang again.

'It must be for me,' he said to Perkins who had moved toward him to be sure he replaced the receiver properly.

She retreated, reluctantly.

'Hello!' he said again, trying to sound put out.

Stijn knew it was Verbrugge, the way he rolled his 'r's when pronouncing 'Bruyne.'

'Be at the Sinclair station on First and Grizzly in ten minutes or do you prefer the authorities find out who you really are … or worse?'

Stijn slammed down the receiver, which startled the woman, and left it askew on one side of the cradle.

'You owe me twenty-five cents!' she demanded crossly, straightening the receiver ...

*

Mrs. Sarah Perkins. Yes, cross and unpleasant, but in rebuttal, life had stolen from her all that had once been soft and loving. Sarah had been happily married until August 25, 1942, when the war (the Japanese) took her Marine husband, Bradley, on Guadalcanal.

After the war, her only child, Daniel (Danny), contracted polio, the doctors told her, at a St. Louis, Missouri, swimming pool. They put Danny in an 'iron lung,' but that gave him only two more months of life.

Nearly bereft of her sanity and all that had been loving inside her, Sarah decided to escape to the sparsely populated Rockies, to any place where she could both keep herself alive and have as little contact with people as possible.

Eventually, she settled on Ennis, Montana, a small town, dependent for its livelihood on local cattle ranchers and tourists. She had quickly seen the value in the tourist trade if not the tourists themselves. Subsequently, she arranged her home, which she bought with her husband's government life insurance, in a manner to provide as little human contact as possible.

The deaths of her husband and child had begun Sarah's steep psychological decline into the person who could see nothing more of value in her guests than to confront them, arms crossed, for 'twenty-five cents.'

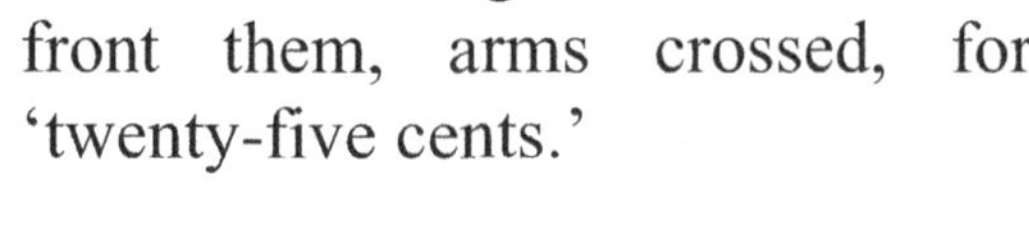

*

Tourist homes offered convenient respites for travelers in the days before ballooning postwar wealth and interstate highways led to an explosion of more roomy, private, and modern motels.

Stijn's room at the Perkins place was old, mildewy and sparsely appointed: bed, dresser, bedside lamp, one rickety chair and a small window with a sash that let in cold air. No closet or table for his canvases. Flowery wallpaper held the entire depressing ensemble together ... sort of.

'Stijn's inhospitable landlady commanded a monopoly of accommodations for the single traveler,' Dan Wiley continued, 'so, she held considerable negotiating leverage. When Stijn came knocking, she assured him with a straight face that he'd find nothing finer in Ennis or anywhere else 'in these parts.''

*

The artist, short that precious quarter of a dollar, sat on the edge of his bed in a cold sweat. He'd been expecting something like this ever since the DP camp, the last time he saw the men from the Utrecht cell. It appeared that Verbrugge and the others, like him, had escaped both Dutch resistance and Allied justice. How? How had they found him? What did they want? What did Verbrugge mean by 'or worse'?

He had little time to answer those questions. It would take five of the allotted ten minutes to walk to the filling station. He was afraid and didn't want to think of the gang at all, especially as to why they were in Ennis. If he could put it all out of his mind, he thought, it would go away. He struggled to think of Marge or his Rotterdam Academy days, the happiest times in his life, but neither ploy worked. The waking nightmare didn't end.

Stijn closed the door to the room where he had spent the past miserable week when he wasn't painting, descended the rickety stairs and began a tremulous walk to the Sinclair station.

19/

F for Fake (1973)

Archie, that phone call suddenly and unexpectedly threatened Stijn's freedom—even his life. After a couple of years in a Displaced Person's camp in Germany and additional years in various parts of the United States, the members of Stijn's Utrecht cell gravitated to Detroit, Michigan, and engaged in a crime spree of minor burglaries. Soon, however, their appetite for more money grew and, commensurately, the focus of their targets switched from the petty to the lucrative art world ...

"Following some preliminary heists with disappointing financial results, Verbrugge, De Coster, Beeks,

Baumann and Pieters hit on a fantastic scheme, their pièce de résistance. To carry it out, however, they needed to find Stijn and enlist his art know-how in service of the caper. They had good reason to believe he would cooperate."

*

He saw them before they did him. They looked different. No more DP livery. Verbrugge wore a brown suit, not inexpensive, a gaudy green and yellow tie and matching brown hat and leather Oxfords.

'Calf leather,' Stijn imagined. 'Soft. That meant money.'

Jeroen Pieters was not so nattily attired: dungarees, red and black plaid shirt and watch cap. He was noticeably pigeon-toed.

'Strange,' he thought. He never spotted that peculiar walk before. Side by side or walking, the pair looked preposterous.

'What did Verbrugge say his new name was? Oh, yeah, 'Teetor.''

Stijn couldn't remember the first name, but in any case, he was sure he'd never use it. He had almost forgotten how much he detested these men.

'Well, well, well. Look what we have here,' Verbrugge said dismissively as Stijn approached the pair. 'Allow me to introduce your old friend, Jero' ...

The 'watch cap' interrupted.

'Hello, Stijn, it's me, 'Delvin Styles.' Used to be Jeroen Pieters. So, you're still De Bruyne?' he wondered aloud. His rhetorical question oozed condescension.

Stijn found 'Styles' haughtiness a bit goofy.

'Yes, but of course I've no reason to change my name. What's your excuse, Pieters?'

Stijn refused to use the man's American name.

'Something shady, I'll bet.'

With that, the gloves were off. There was no hiding it: they didn't like each other. Never did.

'Take it easy, De Bruyne,' Verbrugge said. 'No reason to get uppity. We're here to offer you a chance to make some real money.'

'How did you find me?'

'Mostly by accident. I remembered your interest in western landscapes going back to your days at the Rotterdam Academy. Did you know that one of your Wind River paintings is cited in a catalog of up and coming artists?'

'No, I didn't,' Stijn said truthfully.

'Anyway, we contacted galleries on the East Coast with an interest in western landscapes and ran across that citation. We asked the curators if they'd heard of you and if so, whether they possessed any information about you: addresses, phone numbers … stuff like that. One lady recognized the red rocks in your painting and told us they existed only in the Wind River valley. So, we headed west ...

'On our way to galleries near Yellowstone and the Tetons … You remember that old cabin you painted in Virginia City, just back up the road, over that ridge? We went in there to take a break and have a Coke and guess what? There you were! You must have sold that piece to that store owner, 'cause he displayed it ...

'He told us you left a couple of weeks earlier, headed toward Ennis and the Madison. So, when we got to town, we made inquiries at all the places where you might be staying. There aren't many. It's a small town; didn't take long to find you. Your landlady was very complimentary. Be grateful for her flattery.

'Why have you gone to all this trouble? Why so desperate?'

'Well, my friend, we've been looking for you a long time. We have a proposition; one we believe you can't refuse.'

'What if I do refuse? I'm not interested an any 'proposition' you might offer.'

'Listen to me carefully, De Bruyne. You have been living a lie. You collaborated with the Nazis. That makes you a war criminal! What kind of future as an artist do you think you'll have if we reveal your past, which we will if you refuse to cooperate? I daresay your painting career will be over. The Americans will extradite you to a Nuremberg-style court. There's no statute of limitations on war crimes, you know.'

'You think *you* won't face justice if you do that, Verbrugge? And you, Pieters? There's plenty of evidence I could produce against you and the others! You were much more involved in the *NSB* than I. You have the blood of hundreds of people on your hands. I don't!'

'Don't worry about us.'

Verbrugge smiled slyly.

'The American government knows all about us. How else do you think we have our freedom? No, you won't be able to shift your responsibility for collaboration onto *our* shoulders!'

Verbrugge's assertion staggered Stijn. Questions flooded his mind. How could this be? How could the

American government ignore the crimes committed in Holland and the men responsible for them?

He seemed to have forgotten his own escape from justice.

'What is so important to bring these guys all the way to Montana?'

He didn't have to wait for an answer.

'Look,' Verbrugge said, 'you're coming back to the Madison Motor Court with us. The others—you'll remember them—are waiting there. Then we'll all go down to the Big Hole Café for a nice dinner and discuss a plan we have in mind that will make us all quite rich. You, too, if you play ball.'

The idea of dinner with these men revolted Stijn. But he had to acknowledge that Verbrugge's threat gave the gang leader leverage over him … for the moment.

20/

The Monuments Men (2014)

The trio of former colleagues, who time and circumstance had turned into bitter enemies, walked to the Madison Motor Court and then downtown accompanied by the remaining gang members: De Coster ('Colby'), Beeks ('Brown') and Baumann ('Davis'). Stijn decided he had no choice but to hear what the gang planned, but he would do so without making a commitment of support. He had little choice, but he had begun to fashion a counter strategy.

The Big Hole Café, unlike DuBois's remodeled Red Rock Café, was just what you'd expect of a cheap, downtown eating spot in a small western town. It came as no surprise to Stijn that Verbrugge picked it.

Big Hole customers, it was no exaggeration to say, took their lives into their own hands on entering. There were no finer points with which to contend. They faced gum-popping waitresses with shrill, piercing voices when they weren't busy grinding away; a counter fronting the service area, a cash register at one end near the entrance; wobbly metal stools with cracked, faux-leather red cushions; a half-dozen wooden booths heavily defaced by customers' initials, scatology, and chewing gum stuck underneath; and each booth equipped with a musical Rolodex of songs that played from the jukebox near the entrance.

Stuffed animal heads—deer, elk, moose, boar—cheap landscapes, western trappings, the purpose of which puzzled every customer who wasn't a westerner, and rusty ranch implements adorned the walls. Above everything lay a ceiling of squares of dimpled tin tiles coated with grease, many of them warped or partly detached. In a darkened corner, management had stacked galvanized buckets, apparently intended to catch the rain that seeped through those tiles, the water stains evident. Dim table lamps seemed right at home in this atmosphere, as did the dust and grease-encrusted fluorescent fixtures that dangled ominously from the ceiling by jury-rigged wiring.

Also dangling from the wiring and lamps were a dozen or more old flypaper coils. Thousands of insect carcasses, testament to their utility, were stuck thereon for eternity or until a brave waitress screwed up the courage to remove them.

*

'I want you to read this bulletin from the Frick Museum in New York City, De Bruyne,' Verbrugge instructed over a hardened bread pudding. 'Maybe you've heard of the guys who 'stole' this artwork? We can talk after you've looked it over.'

Verbrugge unfolded a brochure and shoved it at Stijn, who watched it slither across the table. He slowly picked it up, glaring at Verbrugge all the while. Finally satisfied the look of defiance he directed across the table at Verbrugge had made his point, Stijn slowly lowered his eyes and began to read:

> Three hundred and fifty men and women volunteered for military service to protect monuments and other cultural treasures from destruction during World War II. In civilian life many of them were museum directors, curators, artists, architects and educators. These dedicated men and women tracked, located and ultimately returned to their rightful owners more than five million artworks and cultural items stolen by Hitler and the Nazis. Their role in preserving Europe's cultural treasures was without precedent.
>
> Few people are aware that another group of dedicated art historians were engaged in 'the fight for art' on American shores. In 1943 William B. Dinsmoor, a Columbia professor and chairman of the American Council of Learned Societies, established the Committee on the Protection of Cultural Treasures in War Areas. Made up of thirty volunteer American and European scholars, the committee was charged with creating (and distributing to the Allied armed forces) maps and lists of important monuments to be spared during bombing raids.
>
> Headquartered principally at the Frick Art Reference Library, which has been involved in the preservation effort since 1941, Dinsmoor's

> committee was responsible for coordinating information gathered from myriad sources and compiling it into a master index that listed the historic buildings and important works of art in each occupied country.
>
> In 1943 the library closed its doors for six months—the only time in its ninety-three-year history that it has done so—in order to support the committee's research and generate the photography required to prepare more than 700 maps.
>
> Before the end of hostilities the Frick staff and its resources also played a vital role in the research needed for the recovery of stolen and looted art, which became a top priority of Dinsmoor's committee and its parent Washington-based Commission for the Protection and Salvage of Artistic and Historic Monuments in Europe. Researchers—with the help of the Frick Art Reference Library's vast resources—continue to piece together information to help reunite works of art and their rightful owners.

Stijn returned the brochure more politely than it was given to him, although not without a hint of disgust. Perhaps he thought a lesson in manners wouldn't hurt. But it was more the latter than the former, and it did not escape Verbrugge's attention.

'No, I'm not familiar with any of this," Stijn replied finally. "What are the Frick people to me? I've never heard of any of them.'

'Then let me educate you about those so-called rescuers,' Verbrugge said. 'I'm familiar with the reputation of one of them: Craig Hugh Smyth. What a name! Three of them. Reeks of elitism. He is, or was, at the Frick. Smyth was one of those 'rescuers,' and I aim to get revenge for what he and the others did.'

Stijn tried hard to imagine why Smyth's actions were so outrageous to Verbrugge. He thought what they did a matter of justice.

Verbrugge had done his homework. For the next few minutes Stijn listened to his recitation about who stole art from whom.

'The Nazis plundered cultural property from every occupied territory from 1933 until the end of World War II,' Verbrugge said. 'They favored gold but also grabbed silver and currency, cultural items of great significance, including paintings, ceramics, books and religious treasures ...

'Late in 1940 Goering issued an order mandating the seizure of Jewish art collections and other objects because of their significant value. They sent the loot to the Museum Jeu de Paume in Paris. There, art historians and other personnel inventoried the booty before sending it on to Germany ...

'Goering ordered everything divided between Hitler and himself. Whatever the two of them did not covet, they made available to other Nazi leaders ...

'Although the Frick people and other rescuers retrieved most of the items,' Verbrugge explained, 'many are still missing. There is an international effort under way to find that lost art, with the aim, when found, of returning the items to the rightful owners, their families or their respective countries ...

'So, you see, De Bruyne, it's simple. Those guys at the Frick, particularly Smyth, helped to grab all that art, a lot of it Jewish-owned, and return it to the home countries, even to the descendants of Jewish collectors who may be able to claim ownership …

'About the Frick. Their people contributed significantly to the recovery of art in Europe, which they brag about, as you read in that brochure. We're going after their place—turn the tables on them. Your job will be to distinguish the most profitable pieces. After that, the rest of us will go in, nick those and sell as much as we can to the highest bidders. That's it. Simple.'

'So, this is all about some twisted notion of revenge. Some weird form of anti-Semitism.'

Verbrugge didn't take the bait.

'You guys are doing the break in?'

Stijn looked at each man incredulously. Some of them refused to make eye contact with him.

'That's a laugh!' Stijn scoffed. 'You haven't the slightest idea of the preparation involved in that kind of job or how to pull it off. You aren't interested in revenge. You're just a bunch of penny-ante thieves! …

'Have you ever looted a museum or any other secure location? I doubt it and you have no experience fencing stolen art. What do you know about the market for stolen art? Who are your buyers? What's in it for them? Have you ever pulled off a successful job?'

'Yes, we have,' Verbrugge said coyly.

He was lying. The gang never stole art. Instead, their stash came from a series of amateurish strong-arm robberies all the way from New York to Ennis: mom-and-pop grocery stores, liquor stores, gas stations, bars, dark-alley muggings—the sort of thing Thijs Verbrugge first mastered in Utrecht.

Verbrugge looked straight at Stijn, his face expressing supreme confidence in the gang's ability to succeed with the Frick.

'We've learned a lot more since those earlier jobs,' Verbrugge carried on with his bluff, 'and, thus, we're better prepared for this one. With your addition, we can't miss!'

'Where's the loot from those jobs?' Stijn challenged.

'We're sitting on it, but never mind. It's plenty safe.'

That part was true, although Stijn didn't believe a word of it. Verbrugge, he decided, had no grip on reality. The gang's dinner 'guest' concluded that, in any case, Verbrugge would never tell him the truth about anything, so he changed the subject to his own predicament.

'You may think you have leverage with me because of my membership in the *NSB*,' Stijn said, 'but any fear I might have of prosecution won't be enough to persuade me to take part in this hair-brained scheme. Your twisting of the facts I read in that paper is astonishing. I think you've lost your marbles. What's to prevent me from going straight to the authorities?'

'Like I said earlier, you're a war criminal! The Justice Department isn't going to brush that off as easily as you suppose. That's going to keep you from being a rat.'

The antagonists stared at each other, warily, silently.

'Okay, enough for tonight,' Verbrugge announced with a sigh of resignation. 'How are you traveling?' he asked, looking at Stijn.

'Bus and hitching,' Stijn said crisply. He wanted the interview over. He couldn't stand talking or looking at them any longer.

Verbrugge wasn't cooperating.

'Tomorrow, all of us, including you, De Bruyne, are taking a bus to North Dakota and then a train back East, the way we came. In case you try to pull a fast one, like running to the nearest police station, I've got all the persuasion I need in my pocket to prevent that.'

He showed Stijn the butt of a pistol inside his suit coat.

'The other guys are armed, too, he deadpanned.'

The threat seemed real enough, Stijn decided.

'Dinner's on us. We 'invited' you,' Verbrugge said, winking at the gang, a wry smile on his face intended for Stijn.

Verbrugge's sycophants snickered obsequiously.

'After we finish this crappy dessert … what the heck is it … we'll go back to your place and watch you pack up. You're coming over to the motor court with us. You can sleep on the floor.'

That the gang would consider Stijn a second-class member, consigned to the floor, did not surprise him. Rather than rail against the gang's pecking order, however, he decided his focus should be on finding time alone to alert authorities to the gang's plan. As for his vulnerability to the charge of collaboration, all he needed to put that to rest was testimony from Monique or Natan Posner—if they were still alive.

He also knew the plan he had hatched with Marge needed changing. He was headed to New York before he expected but having lost the advantage of timing, he prepared himself mentally to leave, confident he would find a way to outfox the gang and set some form of the DuBois scheme in motion.

21/

The Firm (1993)

The New York Central's '20th Century Limited' steamed steadily, if not speedily, toward its ultimate destination, Manhattan's Grand Central Station. The first morning out of Chicago Stijn found himself alone at a table in the dining car. He looked forward to a quiet, uneventful breakfast.

The car's warm and palatial atmosphere added to his expectancy: oversize silverware and solid plates, vases full of flowers next to carefully folded, starched cloth napkins, all of it arranged with geometric precision on pristine white tablecloths.

The architectural ambiance of the car was of the then-popular art deco style: mirrors etched with train motifs set above windows, the latter crying out for cleaning; wallpaper of boldly delineated, broad horizontal stripes on three-foot protruding walls designed to separate some of the tables. Stijn, however, thought the outcroppings offered only a false sense of privacy.

Temporarily hypnotized by the train's motion and the clickety-clack of the car's wheels as they struck rail after rail, Stijn watched cornfield after cornfield whiz by, a monotony broken only by ugly junk yards, dilapidated fences and other unpleasant manifestations of an impoverished, urban industrial society—the 'wrong' side of the tracks—where the uncaring, well-heeled decided railways and declining property values belonged … far from themselves.

Suddenly refocused, Stijn looked around and satisfied himself the Verbrugge gang was sleeping in. A precious moment of freedom!

*

'May I join you?'

The question and questioner took Stijn by surprise. He looked up into the eyes of a stranger, although he had caught glimpses of him from time to time as the gang made its way east from Dakota.

'That's odd,' he thought but forgot about the connection immediately.

Before Stijn could respond to the stranger's request, he slid into the seat opposite. He wasn't smiling.

'Uh, yes, of course.'

Clearly, Stijn didn't have a choice, but he tried to be polite.

Stijn quickly tried to size up the man now seated across the table. The man seemed so forward—so eager. He appeared older than Stijn and wore in a gray business suit inappropriately cut for the man's solid frame. An off-the-rack ensemble, Stijn wagered. Cheap. Robert Hall?

'I'm sorry to be so abrupt, the man offered with a halfhearted wave that did not excuse his lack of grace, I've been meaning to speak to you for several days, but you always seem cut off from other passengers by those other men. Are they friends of yours?'

'Yes.'

Stijn was being cautious, of course and not particularly mannerly, considering the man's unwanted intrusion.

Recognizing Stijn's reluctance to talk about his 'friends,' the stranger changed the subject.

'What looks good this morning?'

'Just some coffee and oatmeal for me, I think. My usual.'

'What can I get you gentlemen this morning? Some coffee?'

The dining steward's deep, gravely baritone interrupted the pair's stilted conversation. The black man set down two glasses of ice water as he spoke, his free arm draped with a carefully folded white napkin used, Stijn surmised, to clean the glasses before he filled them and before that, the silverware and plates. An immaculate white shirt with starched collar, black tie and a suit coat sandwiched his colorful vest. The ensemble imparted a special dignity to what Stijn knew to be a low-paying job.

The timbre of the man's voice briefly allowed Stijn to imagine him as belonging to a choir, an AME church on Chicago's south side, perhaps, or a barbershop quartet.

Stijn's companion ordered coffee and Stijn his usual.

The two men made small talk about the passing scenery and the upcoming presidential election while waiting for their breakfasts. He 'liked Ike,' the stranger admitted. Stijn didn't have a feel for either candidate, although he knew of Eisenhower's war record. Other than that, there was no reason he should take an interest. He wasn't a citizen and couldn't vote.

*

Suddenly, the stranger stopped talking about scenery and politics and, leaning forward, stared straight into Stijn's eyes, no longer in a convivial manner. The pause before the man spoke seemed an eternity.

'You're in a world of trouble, son,' he said sternly in a voice just above a whisper. 'Frank Borst, FBI.'

The G-Man let that sink in.

'Trouble you can't manage alone. I want to help you if I can. I strongly suggest you let me.'

Stijn collapsed back into his seat. The man's new, ominous demeanor left him little reason to doubt his words.

'Then you know who I am?'

'We've known about you—your past activities in the Netherlands—ever since you entered the country in 1949.'

'Oh, shit! Did he mean my collaboration?' Stijn wondered dejectedly.

'We've been trying to nail your pals for a long time. Did you know they're professional thieves? They began stealing within a year of their arrival, the same year as you. We know they've followed you across the country, but we're not sure why. We think they may be planning something new. Do you know what they might be up to?'

'No,' Stijn lied after pausing.

'Look, De Bruyne. Let me sum up your situation. You help us put these guys away—cooperate, give evidence—and the government will go easier on you. Otherwise, you're looking at a bunch of felonies and that means jail and deportation to The Hague.'

Stijn wanted to be sure he could trust this agent before he said anything more. His hesitation in answering directly may have been a hint to Borst of his guilt. At any rate, Stijn ignored Borst's threat.

'How do I know you're who you say?'

'You think I'm screwing around here, De Bruyne?'

There was no mistaking the clear threat. Stijn gulped but said nothing.

Borst looked around the car as though he weren't, apparently making certain no one was paying attention. Then he reached into his suit, picked up his napkin and fumbled with both in his lap before putting a wrapped package on the table.

'Open it carefully,' he instructed. 'My credentials are in there.'

They were, but his 'badge' wasn't metal. It consisted of two sections displayed horizontally in a leather wallet designed to flip open with one hand. The top half included the agent's name and rank typed across a blue, stylized version of the letters 'FBI,' and the bottom section featured an image of the agent and his signature: 'Frank L. Borst.' Stijn believed he was who he said.

'I'll repeat my question. Do you know if those men are planning a new caper? It's time to start cooperating.'

Just then Stijn saw Verbrugge and the others enter the car. He cleared his throat and tried to convey their presence to the FBI man by rapidly shifting his eyes back and forth. He was thankful there were no free tables near theirs.

Beeks saw Stijn, who had forgotten what the man called himself, but he could not get a good look at Borst whose back was to him. Conveniently, the waiter arrived with coffee and their breakfasts, which lent a welcome air of normality to a scene that might otherwise have looked suspicious.

'You've got to help me get away from them,' Stijn said, just above a whisper.

Borst took his hint.

'I'll think of something,' his nod said.

The G-man sipped a bit of his coffee then excused himself in a manner that made their sitting together appear innocent.

Stijn finished his oatmeal and left the car in the same direction as Borst. He hoped the agent would try to contact him again with an escape plan. Verbrugge saw Stijn get up and he took up pursuit a few feet behind.

In the noisy, rattling vestibule between cars Stijn felt Verbrugge's hand on his shoulder. His powerful grip spun Stijn around. That, plus the train's movement nearly caused Stijn to fall.

'Who was that guy, De Bruyne?'

It was difficult to hear.

'Don't know, really. All I know is he introduced himself by a last name … 'Allen,' I think it was,' Stijn shouted. 'He didn't want to talk. Just drank some of his coffee and left. Maybe he needed the WC?' Stijn suggested with a grin, hoping to deflect Verbrugge's suspicion.

The gang leader didn't laugh.

'Get back to your compartment,' he ordered. He meant the one Stijn shared with Baumann that adjoined Verbrugge's. He followed Stijn closely through two cars. Stijn could feel Verbrugge's breath on the back of his neck.

'He had something with garlic for breakfast,' Stijn surmised.

22/

Throw Momma from the Train (1987)

Stijn thought it was around three that afternoon when he heard a wailing siren in the distance and felt the sudden jolt and deceleration caused by the train's emergency braking system. Had he not been sitting, he would have lost his balance. A loud commotion in the corridor outside his compartment followed the siren.

Stijn poked his head out the door just as the porter came by, politely pushing passengers aside to get through the congestion.

'Porter! What's happened?'

'Not sure, sir,' he yelled over the din. 'One of the passengers said someone fell or jumped from the train.

I'm going to check with the conductor in the last car. He radioed about seeing a man in a gray suit lying alongside the track. We're stopping to investigate.'

'Where are we?'

'Somewhere west of Toledo, I'd guess,' the porter said before finally disappearing down the crowded corridor.

Minutes later Stijn saw dozens of uniformed police and several men in civilian clothes outside his window. The latter began boarding the train. The porter returned with a report: someone fell, or someone pushed someone off the train, and the police were checking everyone's identity.

Two of the men in civilian attire knocked at Stijn's compartment. Verbrugge was there with the others, who were back by then. The detectives checked all their tickets and moved on.

Hours later the train still stood where it stopped. Baumann and Stijn spent the time playing pinochle.

Then, a knock at their door. Before they could reply two other detectives entered. They produced credentials identical to Borst's.

'Mr. Stijn De Bruyne?'

'Yes,' Stijn answered.

'FBI. Come with us. We have some questions.'

Baumann said nothing but threw a glance toward the door to Verbrugge's berth.

Stijn agreed to go along. When the three of them reached the corridor, Verbrugge emerged from his compartment.

'What's going on, gentlemen?' he said, looking at the agents.

'We're taking this man along for questioning. What business of that is yours?'

The curt dismissal flummoxed Verbrugge.

'None, none, of course. Thanks,' he sputtered and stood aside.

The two FBI men escorted Stijn from the train to a waiting automobile. One of them finally introduced himself as Robert Greenleaf. He did all the talking.

*

Robert Ludlow Greenleaf was a twenty-year veteran of the Bureau. Born in Charleston, South Carolina and educated at the Citadel, Greenleaf joined the FBI fresh out of Harvard Law School. His marks there were decidedly undistinguished. And because he came to the Bureau just after the end of Prohibition in 1933, he hadn't the experience of more seasoned agents who earned their stripes and the Director J. Edgar Hoover's plaudits by successfully pursuing bootleg gangsters and bank robbers across the country.

Instead, Greenleaf's indoctrination to the operational rationales and methods of the FBI came during the war when he became an instrumental arm of the Bureau and Director J. Edgar Hoover by investigating and rounding up suspicious Italian and German aliens on the East Coast. A role in Hoover's Anti-Communist crusade lay just ahead.

Greenleaf's investigative experience also gave him entrée to the ways and means of the New Jersey Mob and its elusive North Caldwell don. Greenleaf knew that many of the dons and their immediate subordinates, men with real money to spend and huge appetites for expensive original art.

*

'Relax, De Bruyne,' Greenleaf said, although to De Bruyne didn't think it genuine. He decided to be wary of further attempts at flattery or congenial cajoling.

'After your breakfast with Agent Borst, the Bureau arranged this ruse to get you away from the gang. Borst is fine. Another of our agents, a very much younger and athletic one, jumped from the train and pretended to be dead. We needed to talk to you about Verbrugge's plans, not about a 'murder' …

'After a reasonable delay, we'll re-board you and float a rumor that you were a 'person of interest' because you sat for breakfast with Borst, the 'murdered' man. In the meantime, the police will have discovered the real 'culprit,' another agent, hiding in a compartment closet in another car. That should satisfy the gang's curiosity about your brief disappearance ...

'Now, let's get down to it. Is the gang planning a new theft?'

'Yes!' Stijn burst out without thinking over what had just been asked. He was simply relieved to be out from under the gang's control, but had he moved from one form of control to another? He decided to cooperate until he felt he couldn't.

'I'm ready to cooperate based on Agent Borst's offer to me if I helped the government."

The agents shared smiles of satisfaction.

'They think they can steal paintings from the Frick Museum in New York. They want revenge for the rescue of art stolen by the Nazis and returned to state-owned galleries or Jewish owners. The Frick comes into the picture because several experts from the Frick gave valuable help to the people involved in rescuing the art ...

'Much of the art the Nazis stole belonged to Jews and these guys—Nazis, really—hate Jews. They became collaborators in Holland for precisely that reason. My opinion? I think they're just a bunch of thieves.'

'Whew! The Frick? Seriously?' Greenleaf exclaimed. 'The jobs we believe they've pulled off before can't compared to the complexity of this one. What do they want from you?'

'I'm supposed to identify the valuable pieces; small ones that can easily be removed and fenced. I told them they were crazy.'

'What's their hold over you? Why should they think you'd cooperate?'

Stijn hesitated, then realized he would lose nothing by fessing up.

'I joined their cell in Utrecht because I was hiding a Jewish family in my attic. The Resistance thought that would end any suspicion. I was a patriot and wanted to do something! Verbrugge is blackmailing me. They believe the threat of my exposure as a collaborator will persuade me to help.'

'You have proof of that you were hiding Jews?'

'Not exactly. After liberation, I don't know what happened to the family I secreted in my attic, and the same for my Resistance contact, a woman named Monique Schoepp. She was the sister of the Resistance contact who persuaded me to take in the Posner family. I knew the father, Natan Posner, from our days at the art academy. Monique knew I had hidden the family. She or Natan could support my claim ...

'So, I'm in an impossible situation. If I refuse to help in the robbery, they'll expose me, and the Americans will deport me to Holland for prosecution. If I do help them, there's a strong possibility of failure with the same result. However, if I have witnesses to testify to my deception, Verbrugge will have no hold over me. How you stop the robbery is up to you.'

'Well, not entirely up to us,' Greenleaf said. 'We have known about your 'collaboration' for some time. What we didn't understand was the reason behind it. You did a courageous thing …

'But, if you want to come out of this with your life and reputation restored, you'll have to help us catch these guys. You won't like the alternative. So, I'm going to explain how you can help, but I must warn you that doing so may be quite dangerous. What do you say?'

Stijn hesitated again. He recognized the FBI was also blackmailing him, but he didn't see any alternative other than to cooperate.

'I'll do as you ask,' he said with a sigh.

'Okay. We'll put you back on the train. The passengers will learn the person guilty of killing Borst is under arrest ...

'You're to continue on to New York with the gang. When I've finished, Charlie,' Greenleaf pointed to his partner, Charles Freeman, 'will explain our method of contacting you and you us. It involves signals and message drops. That way we'll know everything the gang is up to ...

'You're to play along throughout the operation's planning and execution. At the last moment, on a signal from you, we'll close in and catch them red-handed. Once we have them behind bars that will clear you of any wrongdoing and you'll be on your way.'

Greenleaf turned to Freeman and the two talked in whispers for several seconds. Stijn wondered if his story had cleared him, although he hadn't provided any verification of his claim about the Posners. He got his answer.

'We'll attempt to locate the Posners and Monique Schoepp. The government has information and methods to draw on that you don't.'

While Greenleaf spoke to someone on the car radio, agent Freeman took Stijn aside and explained the communication methods employed by the FBI. Then they put him back on the train.

*

Stijn, it turned out, had nothing to fear from the gang when he rejoined them. Verbrugge and his cohorts bought the phony story about Borst's 'demise' and accepted Stijn back like a conquering hero, their disdain for police heavy handedness and incompetence thoroughly vindicated by his false detention.

*

The '20th Century Limited' left Albany, New York, a half hour late. Much to Stijn's delight and relief, the engineer roared down the Hudson Valley, whipping around the curves and through the local stations—Stijn was always a bit of a thrill seeker—bolting into Harmon, where the station crew broke its own speed records hooking up the electric locomotive that brought them into Grand Central on time.

23/

Dirty Rotten Scoundrels (1988)

In the dining commons at *Renaissance,* Archie asked Dan to hold off on the narrative long enough for an observation and questions that'd been bothering him since Stijn met up with the Verbrugge gang in Ennis.

"Dan, this business about a proposed robbery seemed to reveal somethin' about Stijn's character different from what we learned about his behavior durin' the war and out West. And I'd bet the deal he made with Marge Balfour also involved somethin' unsavory or criminal. Aren't there two different stories here and two different 'Stijns'? How are we supposed to make sense of that?"

"Well, I think it's possible, maybe even justifiable, to see Stijn as having a 'Jekyll and Hyde' personality. But that's not certain ...

"I think Stijn told me all that stuff about the war to boost my opinion of his character. He realized that later his part in the robbery would make him look like a common criminal."

"But Dan, didn't you ever ask him about this? You two must have talked for hours."

"I didn't, Archie and I regret that, of course. I thought if I pressed him on delicate, embarrassing topics, he'd clam up. I wasn't sure his story about hiding the Posners was true. And if it weren't true, that would leave only one 'Stijn.' It might have been different if I'd had some training as a reporter, knowing the right questions, when to press and when not ...

"Whatever you decide, Archie, remember this: Stijn's was a *story*! Maybe he thought an ambiguous identity would create more interest. That is always the point of a story, right? Stories are just that … *stories*. Are they true? Maybe. Somewhat true? Probably. Embellished? Sure. Lies? Quite possibly."

"Yeah, I see what you're saying, Dan. The story definitely has me hooked, just as you predicted, and tryin' to figure out who or what Stijn's true make-up was a big part of it—a challenge."

"There's one more thing you should consider, Archie. You don't know the rest of the story, so you'll have to live with your questions, your doubts, until the end. There may be no satisfactory resolution. No happy conclusion. Nothing black or white. I *absolutely* believe when I've finished you won't think of these characters as either simple or predictable. Maybe that's what Stijn wanted us to understand. Or maybe he just wanted us to enjoy the story without philosophizing about it ...

"Okay, everybody? If you're ready, I'll continue."

*

Verbrugge seemed to have an endless supply of cash. Among many examples of his largess in New York City, he rented a suite of rooms for the gang at the Franklin Hotel on Manhattan's Upper East Side at 164 E. 87th Street. This should have caused Stijn to wonder about the source of Verbrugge's stash. He did, but he decided that doing so would only increase the tension between the two of them. At this point it didn't seem to matter which illegal activities generated the money.

His choice of the Franklin, Verbrugge argued, gave the gang an ideal perch from which to keep an eye on the routines of museum staff, particularly the security guards and close enough to carry tools to the Frick—by hand if necessary. It was still unclear how the gang would move the art once they liberated it from the gallery walls.

*

To explain why the gang needed so much space at the hotel, Verbrugge told the manager the troop was from

Hollywood, scouting locations for a movie. He even gave gang members with casual wardrobes befitting his notion of southern California dress. Stijn played along. He liked the colorful cravats that tucked into his shirts, and he always left the top button undone to show off as much of the neckwear as possible. Verbrugge assigned Stijn the role of 'scriptwriter.' So, to complete his new persona, as he imagined it, Stijn added a handsome meerschaum pipe he found at a neighborhood smoke shop.

Stijn, of course, didn't know the first thing about the look of a scriptwriter, otherwise he would have chosen a less flamboyant getup. He figured other guests, and the hotel staff would have no better idea what a scriptwriter should look like than he.

It took only a few days for two of the guys to find girlfriends. How the newcomers would fit into the Frick plan, if at all, wasn't clear, but they proved to be useful, doing those things that women—mostly—do: laundry, ironing and bed making.

Verbrugge preferred not to engage the hotel staff for such domestic chores, and he had to overcome strenuous objections to the irregularities from the manager. Verbrugge wanted to keep as much anonymity as possible and he succeeded.

They took most of their breakfasts at the hotel, but there were ventures into the neighborhood for midday and evening meals that gave Stijn his first opportunity to experiment with other New York fare. He developed an instant affinity for Chinese restaurants, having never sampled one in Holland.

*

Planning for the break-in continued. The gang considered disguising themselves as security guards and possibly New York police officers. For that, however, they needed authentic-looking uniforms. Verbrugge bought a camera and began to photograph the guards surreptitiously as they went in and out of the museum. It was simple to get police officers on film. Photography was the easy part of the plan.

They couldn't just waltz into a uniform shop and order genuine ensembles. Verbrugge, however, learned techniques for fabricating uniforms during his wartime sparring with the Dutch Resistance. The Resistance, in turn, changed its techniques based on information given them by escaped Allied POWs. With that storehouse of knowledge to draw on, Verbrugge assigned De Coster and Beaks' girlfriends to fashion the phony uniforms using his photos as a blueprint.

The would-be thieves also needed tools should they change their minds about fake guards and try a physical break-in. Verbrugge assigned De Bruyne and himself to get the hardware: hammers, saws, chisels, screwdrivers, crowbars—even an acetylene torch. Eventually, Verbrugge bought a used car from a loud, sleazy salesman he saw on television, a '53, four-door Ford, as Stijn recalled.

The would-be thieves also needed devices to remove the paintings from their frames should that prove necessary. The shoppers found art stores in three different neighborhoods. De Coster, Baumann and Beeks picked one shop per man. On Stijn's advice each took along a list that included Exacto knives to cut through the canvasses and acid-free paper in which to roll them up. Verbrugge also instructed them to look for any books, brochures or pamphlets describing the Frick collection and turn them over to Stijn.

While the trio shopped Stijn walked to the New York Public Library in search of art history. He found more than he could have imagined or digested in the time allotted. So, he decided to focus principally on the artists themselves, believing the value of a painting started with their genius. The size of potential works was critical from a practical sense and that helped to narrow his research further. Then he toured the Frick to admire the paintings he just studied.

24/

On the Waterfront (1954)

An abbreviated biography of Henry Clay Frick, say, in The Encyclopedia Britannica, might read:

'Late 19th century industrialist, financier, union-buster and art patron.'

"The brevity of that imaginary introduction doesn't do justice to the man's life," Dan suggested. "But let's pretend that we have The Britannica in front of us, and from it we can make something of the man's life for ourselves. Agreed, Archie? And the rest of you?"

A small group had pulled up chairs next to and behind Archie. All nodded or verbalized their agreement.

"Okay, then. I'll begin reading aloud."

Dan's imaginary reading, and his combining it with Stijn's story, depicted Frick as an interesting man, and a successful one if measured traditionally. But that didn't make him admirable in everyone's view, as the crisp Britannica bio suggests it should. Include Thijs Verbrugge among the skeptical.

As Verbrugge's gang planned to heist valuable art from New York's Frick Museum, it would seem appropriate to know something more about the museum's patron and the reasons the gang targeted it. The events of World War II may not answer all those questions.

*

The Britannica piece should have included these other facts. Henry Frick founded the H.C. Frick & Company (coke manufacturing company); became chairman of the Carnegie Steel Company; and played a significant role in the formation of the U.S. Steel corporation. He financed construction of the Pennsylvania Railroad and the Reading Company and had extensive real estate holdings in Pittsburgh and throughout the state of Pennsylvania.

His accomplishments didn't stop there. He built the historic, neoclassical Frick Mansion (a landmark building in Manhattan), and on his death in 1919 donated his extensive collection of old master paintings and fine furniture to create the celebrated Frick Collection and art museum.

*

In 1871, at 21 years old, Frick joined with two cousins and a friend in a small partnership that used the beehive oven to turn coal into coke for use in steel manufacturing and vowed to be a millionaire before he turned thirty. He succeeded. By then, the Frick Coke Company had cornered most of the coke business in Pennsylvania.

They manufactured coke by burning off the unstable elements in coal in 'beehive ovens,' making it a reliable, high-intensity fuel abundant and inexpensive to produce. Coke is a gray, hard and porous fuel with a high carbon content and few impurities, made by heating coal or oil in the absence of air.

Although it made a top-quality fuel, coking poisoned the surrounding landscape. After 1900, the serious environmental damage of beehive coking attracted national notice, although the damage, complete destruction of vegetation, had plagued the district for decades. One observer reported that beehive ovens made the entire region of coke manufacture turned the sky 'cheerless and unhealthful.' (Compare the beehive oven to the more recent but defunct 'teepee burner' for incinerating the slash from lumbering operations.)

Thanks to loans from the family friends Frick eventually bought out the partnership and it became H. C. Frick & Company.

*

In the early 1880s Frick's company joined Andrew Carnegie's steel company. The merged companies became a vertically integrated enterprise that later provided Frick with a steady buyer and furnished Carnegie's steel company with a steady source of fuel. Together, these enterprises grew rapidly and, in the process, made Frick and Carnegie two of the wealthiest men in America.

These incredibly wealthy men gave some of their considerable treasure back to the communities in the form of art (Frick), education (John D. Rockefeller bankrolled the University of Chicago), art & history (J.P. Morgan to the Metropolitan Museum and his home is the Morgan Library & Museum) and libraries (Andrew Carnegie gifts helped start about half the public libraries in the United States).

*

Frick's collection reflected the aspirations of the high society into which he was moving. Then, in 1906, Frick took a step to preserve his ever-growing art collection for future generations: he bought the lot at the corner of Fifth Avenue and 70th Street so that he could have a grand mansion of his own.

Not only was Frick himself a polarizing figure—he was known in some circles as the 'the most hated man in America' due to the violence of his union-busting activities—but the construction of his mansion a century ago raised the hackles of New York's Fifth Avenue elite. Nonetheless, Frick continued to live at both his New York mansion and at Clayton until his death.

*

The Frick Collection was home to one of the finest collections of European paintings in the United States. It had many works of art dating from the pre-Renaissance up to the post-Impressionist eras, but in no logical or chronological order. It included several large paintings by J.M.W. Turner and John Constable. In addition to paintings, it also had an exhibition of carpets, porcelain, sculptures, and period furniture.

Any museum attached to Henry Clay Frick was destined to invite controversy.

*

Before he could pursue his dream, misfortune began to hound Frick. As a founding member of the private

South Fork Fishing and Hunting Club on Lake Conemaugh near Pittsburgh, Frick helped found. He was in large part responsible for alterations to the dam.

On May 31, 1889, the dam failed, sending millions of gallons of water downriver toward Johnstown, Pennsylvania. The 2,209 people left dead in its wake made 'Johnstown' the worst disaster in American history. Though Frick quickly set up a relief fund for the victims' families, he couldn't fully dodge the club's—or his own—blame in the tragedy.

*

A national scandal followed when Carnegie Steel workers in Homestead, Pennsylvania, went on strike over issues related to working conditions, fair pay and health hazards, and, significantly, to Frick's vehement opposition to unions and his ongoing attempts to break them. On July 6, 1892, a battle broke out between steelworkers and the Pinkerton agents Frick contracted to reopen the mill. Nine union members and three Pinkerton agents died in the skirmish.

In retaliation, an anarchist burst into Frick's office two weeks later and shot him twice at close range. Remarkably, Frick not only survived the attack but returned to his desk within the week.

*

Henry Clay Frick died of a heart attack in December 1919. From the grave, as it had been from life, he did not hear the people who spoke well or ill of him. Perhaps many critics took a different view of Frick when they learned the house and art collection would become a museum to encourage and develop the study of the fine arts and of advancing knowledge of like subjects.

Adelaide Frick outlived her husband by twelve years.

25/

Entrapment (1999)

Stijn's solo trips from the hotel provided him opportunities to contact the FBI using a technique explained in detail by Charles Freeman back in Ohio. The FBI assumed the gang would hole up near the Frick and close to Central Park.

There are poorly maintained benches—their forest green paint flaking off—on the west side of the model boat lake, a distance from the museum of about four to five blocks.

When Stijn needed to meet with an agent, Freeman instructed him to mark the left end of a wooden back slat—second from the top—with a chalk circle. An agent would put a slash through the circle within twenty-four hours, a signal that Stijn should look for a dark green Chevrolet parked in front of the church of St. Ignatius Loyola on the corner of Park and East 84th, four blocks from the Franklin.

Stijn walked over to the park after completing his visit to the Frick, selected a bench and left his mark. He hoped to free himself of Verbrugge's smothering control during the next couple of days to check for a responding slash.

*

His research and messaging complete, Stijn returned to the hotel to brief Verbrugge on museum security, the art market, potential collectors, and fencing. Verbrugge listened attentively. Perhaps he realized the Frick might be an undertaking beyond anything he allegedly pulled off before.

'Let's begin with the least desirable method, Stijn said, 'which would be to wait until after the heist to fence the paintings. We'd certainly have the art, but we couldn't be sure of our buyers' identities or the market value. It would also be dangerous to seek buyers after the heist for another reason. How could we be sure of their discretion? They might turn us in, or the FBI might be among them ...!

'We must find our buyers before we take the paintings to avoid the exposure inherent in an open market. At some point, I will recommend some prospective buyers. Trust me. I'll know who to ask about that when the time comes. In any case, we'll have to rely on the self-interest of buyers to protect them and us ...

'There are still plusses and minuses. Here's a hypothetical scenario. A prospective buyer is looking for a specific Vermeer and hires some guys to get it. Us, for example. We may also grab a few other works while we're at it, either to throw investigators off track or to provide a little extra money. However, if we take only the Vermeer it will give investigators a short list of those likely end up with it. Professionals know where the interest in a Vermeer lies ...

'There's more. When thieves snatch art of significant value, they rarely sell it outright but use it instead as collateral for loans, arms or drug trade or it circulates within the underworld: the head of a heroin ring with expensive, often gaudy tastes, a Mafioso or some reclusive billionaire. These guys have plenty of money, but they can never show or display the art. All they can do is look at it. The value to them is knowing they have something exquisite and desirable—like owning the Hope Diamond or England's Crown Jewels. You can't do anything with such treasures—you just have them ...

'Still more. Some of the Frick pieces are so valuable they're not insured. Those would be attractive to people like you, given they are small enough to transport easily and we find a trustworthy buyer ahead of time. Once we have the paintings, we can suggest a price, but the buyer will want to bargain. If we sell one for ten percent of its value it will not be to the collector or buyer behind the scene, but to another criminal, a middleman who will sell or trade it for twenty percent to one of the types of people I just named or use it for collateral ...

'If the selling price is in the tens or hundreds of thousands, even millions or a billion or more … Well, you see where I'm going. You get the idea. Jackpot ...!

'We could also sell the paintings as fakes. The easiest and most common way to make money from stolen masterpieces is to sell the real thing on the open market as a very high-quality replica. The thieves will get far less than what it's worth, but when the original is worth 10 or 20 million dollars, they walk away with a nice profit. Many stolen masterpieces are sitting in the collections of legitimate buyers who think the work is a fake ...

'It is extremely difficult to sell the most famous and valuable works without getting caught, since any interested buyer will almost certainly know the work is stolen and advertising it risks someone contacting the authorities ...

'It is also difficult for the buyer to display the work to visitors without it being recognized as stolen, thus defeating much of the point of owning it. Thieves have held many famous works for ransom from the legitimate owner or even returned without a payoff due to the lack of black-market customers. There is no black market for million-dollar paintings. Period. It's not the same thing as a stolen car that you can chop up and resell. When you try to sell it, that's when they get you ...

'Those who steal antiquities and lower-value artworks can often profit from them, but those who take famous paintings can only hope to ransom them with insurers, a risky gambit, likely to fail. Many thieves don't even think that far ahead ...

'Returning a painting for ransom also risks a sting operation. The only buyers for famous artwork might be undercover cops.'

Verbrugge jumped in. He had been fidgeting ever since Stijn began his explanation of options.

'Okay, but how do we find buyers? Were any of the paintings you're considering auctioned to the Frick? If so, wouldn't that give us some idea of their value?'

'Not at all! Normally, museum paintings are either bequests by genuine patrons—art lovers—or tax write-offs for sincere patrons as well as the more cynical ones. Tax write-offs are dangerous, of course, because they invite immediate scrutiny from the IRS ...

'You raised the possibility of getting information about potential clients from earlier auctions. You can't find buyers due to their interest in earlier auctions. W keep bidders names anonymous, except very rarely when mentioned in a newspaper article, but you could never get that information from an auction house or any archive ...

'These buyers—not the sleazy or marginal types I mentioned before—are wealthy, prominent, primarily law-abiding citizens, so you would either strike out or be ratted out by nearly every one of them.

'What's to keep them from turning us in after the exchange?' Verbrugge asked.

'If they've participated in a crime they're not going to talk about it! You could also threaten to kill them, but if you threaten to kill a billionaire who is buying your stolen art, he will either walk away or do the deal … and then have *you* killed! …

'The danger doesn't end there. The second the theft occurs; sophisticated investigation and tracking will begin. The FBI will be poking around the Frick, looking for witnesses, finger and footprints, and the media will print images of the stolen paintings. They would be hot forever ...

'On the other hand, while most high-profile museums have extremely tight security, many places with multi-millions devoted to art have disproportionately poor security measures. They're susceptible to thefts slightly more complicated than a typical smash-and-grab and offer a greater payoff ...

'If all of this sounds complicated and dangerous and I would argue that it is both, I have a couple of alternative suggestions ...

'First, what if, as I mentioned previously, we replace the genuine Frick paintings with forgeries—provided someone *could* forge them—to delay the discovery of the loss and give ourselves some time and cover to dispose of them? …

'Second, we should also consider taking only small paintings. Valuable art pieces are worth millions of dollars and weigh only a few kilograms. So, transporting the booty is not complicated if we're willing to accept some damage to the paintings while cutting them out of their frames and rolling them up in a tube carrier.'

'So, stealing is the easy part,' Verbrugge concluded with a touch of sarcasm. 'We'll find buyers,' he lectured Stijn, 'without doubt and they won't be cops! …

'I'll take what you've told me back to the others. As you instructed, the guys are looking for knives, acid free paper, and tubes at those art shops. You get busy finding us some buyers.'

With that, he slapped Stijn on the back and walked away. His casual manner caused Stijn to wonder whether Verbrugge took seriously of what he had said.

26/

The Thomas Crown Affair (1968)

Stijn penned a condescending note to Verbrugge to which he attached a 'shopping list' of potential plunder. The note amounted to a primer to a mini art history course: a comprehensive description of each piece and its reputation in the art world. Stijn figured that would be important when Verbrugge looked to fence the pieces. He hoped his analysis would end his role in the intended theft:

'Thijs, I know you're not particularly interested in the background of these paintings or of the artists, but I'm going to write out the information for you anyway. I think you should appreciate something about the objects you're stealing. A practical matter: their size also influenced my selections ...

'One more thing: neither I nor anyone else could possibly create convincing forgeries of these works ...

'1. **Piero della Francesca**, (1411/13–1492), An Augustinian Friar (1454–1469), approx. 16 x 11 in. ...

(Thijs, Note the size of each work. Very important.)

'Art historians recognize Piero della Francesca (normally just 'Piero') as one of the great masters of the early Italian Renaissance. He was born between the years 1411 and 1413 in Borgo Santo Sepolcro (Sansepolcro) in eastern Tuscany. His works were primarily frescos that got him commissions from the Pope and prominent Renaissance patrons ...

'Art historians point to his pioneering use of oil paint, his dexterity with light and color, and his ability to execute figures, which are both present and otherworldly. The Augustinian Friar is one of the best examples of this ...

*

'In 1454 a third party commissioned the artist to make a large, three-panel polyptych for the Augustinian monks' high altar in Sansepolcro. He structured the St Agostino altarpiece with a large central panel flanked by panels depicting saints, surrounded by a few smaller panels ...

'Helen Clay Frick, the daughter of Henry, pursued Piero's works for decades before getting the first panel of the altarpiece, St John the Evangelist in 1936—a purchase that created a media frenzy in New York ...

'Helen Frick actively expanded her father's legacy and encouraged the acquisitions of the Augustinian Friar and the Augustinian Nun ...

*

'2. **Jan van Eyck** (ca. 1395–1441), <u>Virgin and Child, with Saints and Donor</u> (ca. 1441–1443), approx. 18 ½ x 24 in. ...

'Specialists believe this work is one of Van Eyck's last paintings but likely finished by his workshop; that is, by an assistant. Nonetheless, it shows the skills that made Van Eyck famous ...

'The virgin and child are both blonde, as they are in most northern European art, and Mary is regally attired standing beneath a brocade canopy – inscribed AVE GRATIA PLENA (Hail Mary, full of grace)—and on an imported carpet laid on a decorative tile floor. It reflects both the material wealth of 15th-century Netherlandish society and van Eyck's exceptional copyist skill ...

'Art historians credit Van Eyck with the invention of and popularization of oil painting, using oil to bind pigment ...

'His naturalism, which showed the experience of everyday life, amazed viewers. Van Eyck used this technique to invite the eye into the image ...

*

'3. **Claude Monet** (1840–1926), <u>Vétheuil in Winter, 1878–1879</u>, approx. 27 x 35 in. ...

'Claude Monet was among the leaders of the French Impressionist movement of the 1870s and 1880s ...

'The Realists' interests in depicting the qualities of nature inspired Monet. Later, he brought the technique to his observations of the same subject at various times of the day ...

'Following the path initiated by Edouard Manet, Monet experimented with bold color and unconventional compositions. The emphasis in his pictures belonged to the qualities of light and color and the atmosphere ...

'Monet painted Vétheuil from different points of view and in every season: from the riverbanks, the meadows and a boat he arranged as a floating studio ...

'Compared to the detailed work of Van Eyck and Vermeer, *Vétheuil in Winter* is a highly impressionistic work ...

*

'4. **Johannes Vermeer** (1632–1675), Officer and Laughing Girl (ca. 1657), approx. 20 x 18 in. ...

'*Officer and Laughing Girl* is typical of most Dutch work at the time and includes many of the characteristics of Vermeer's style. The main subject is the woman and soft, direct light falls on her face ...

'The man in the painting is a cavalier. His red coat and expensive hat show his wealth, rank, power, and passion and add an emotional mood to the painting. The black sash he wears shows him to be an officer and his striking presence adds drama and mystery to the composition ...

'The artistic device, in which the artist places an object in the foreground, increases the depth of field. Vermeer probably used a camera obscura to help create this look. Like the modern camera it projects an image through an aperture into a dark chamber ...

'The window and lighting are characteristic of Vermeer's interior paintings. The glass in the window has many variations of color, showing Vermeer's precision in painting details. Only bright light comes in from the window; no outside scene is ever visible.'

*

Verbrugge took one look at Stijn's 'lecture' on art history and tossed it contemptuously into a wastebasket with an audible curse. Not, however, before he wrote down the titles of the four works described.

27/

Sneakers (1992)

The day after Stijn's dissertation on how to profitably dispose of stolen art and Verbrugge's subsequent tantrum, Stijn told the gang's leader he needed to return to the Frick for a promised tour led by a docent. Verbrugge reluctantly agreed, concluding, Stijn supposed, the gang needed as much inside information as possible. Perhaps he should have been less accommodating. Stijn's true purpose was a rendezvous with the FBI.

Based on Verbrugge's reluctance to let him go, Stijn expected someone to follow him. As he walked along, often pausing to window shop, tie his shoe and other distractions, he saw no one suspicious.

Still, rather than going straight to the park bench, Stijn re-entered the Frick and stayed for a couple of hours, trying to discourage anyone Verbrugge might have dispatched.

Confident no one had tailed him but cautious just the same, Stijn casually strolled along Central Park's walkways, stopping occasionally to offer a friendly 'Hello!' to other walkers—a greeting that astonished them, this being New York—before he reached the bench at the model boat lake. The slashed circle was there!

Stijn left the park, picking up his pace to the church corner, still confident of his anonymity. Then he spotted it! A dark green, two-door Chevrolet, with two men inside.

As Stijn approached, the man on the passenger side opened his door, stepped onto the sidewalk, and pulled the back of his seat forward to open the rear. He motioned Stijn inside without a word.

Agent Greenleaf sat behind the wheel. Once seated, Greenleaf spoke to Stijn via the rearview mirror.

'Mr. De Bruyne, meet Agent Holden.'

Holden had resumed his place in the passenger seat and closed his door.

Stijn nodded and mumbled a greeting in the direction of Holden, who neither turned to look at him nor bothered to acknowledge the introduction. Strange, Stijn thought. Greenleaf started the engine, and they were off.

Greenleaf wasted no time.

'What do you have for us?'

'They're going to hit the Frick. They're buying supplies and have me scouting the place. I tried to warn Verbrugge about the difficulties, not simply of pulling off the heist but of successfully disposing of the loot afterward. I suspect he didn't take me seriously. He reserves seriousness for himself.'

'What's their timing?'

'I can't tell you when they plan to make their move, but it will likely involve fake security guards and/or policemen. Verbrugge has a couple of women—girlfriends of his guys—working on fake uniforms.'

'We figured that's what they'd do,' Greenleaf mused aloud, and Holden jotted down some notes. 'No problem. We'll be ready for that, and all the other stunts guys like them pull, but we need you to update us, especially when it's a 'go.''

'Yeah, sure. But getting away from them to contact you is difficult. I'm all out of excuses. By the way, how is Agent Borst?'

'Oh, he's fine. Remember, he wasn't the one who jumped off the train!'

Stijn felt foolish.

'Of course. Sorry.'

Recovering his dignity, momentarily in disarray, Stijn pressed on.

'Do you know if anyone has located Monique Schoepp or the Posners?'

'We have no information about that. It's in the hands of the State Department. They have their hands full and enjoy limited resources for that. I'm sure something will eventually turn up.'

'It'd better. That's my only ticket out of this mess.'

'Okay, De Bruyne, but next time in the park use one of the benches at the Untermyer Fountain. That's all the way up to the level of 106th Street. We'll change drops after every meeting. Got it?'

'Yeah, sure.'

'We'll let you out in front of St. Ignatius Loyola at Park and 84th.'

Holden said nothing the entire time. Maybe he's an apprentice, Stijn surmised.

*

It was a short walk from the church to the hotel. Verbrugge was waiting for Stijn in the lobby.

'How'd the tour go,' he asked, not curiously but unpleasantly.

Stijn couldn't tell from his look or tone if he was suspicious. The question sounded a bit sarcastic.

'Very well. I've located the paintings.'

'What about security stations and the guards' routine?'

'The guards seemed stationary. Sat on chairs. Looked half asleep. No shift changes during my visit. I have no idea about nighttime. I assume we're going in at night?'

'Yeah, of course,' Verbrugge said nonchalantly.

'I took a floor plan. Whenever you're ready I can show you every security station.'

'The guards armed?'

'No.'

'Okay. Let's give it a rest for now, meet up with the others and head for some dinner. Whadaya say?'

'Fine. I'm ready. All that walking has left me famished.'

With that, both returned to their rooms to wash up.

*

Later that evening Stijn saw Beeks enter Verbrugge's room. From the man's furtive behavior when he saw Stijn down the hall and just before he disappeared inside, Stijn guessed the visit had something to do with him. Despite all the precautions he took, Stijn sensed someone had followed him that afternoon. Minutes after Beeks closed the door Stijn tiptoed to it and overheard a conversation that confirmed his worst fears.

'De Bruyne tried every trick in the book,' he heard Beeks say, 'but I stuck to him until the end. He went to the museum all right, but after that he strolled through the park and sat briefly on a bench near one of those ponds ...

'Then comes the suspicious part, boss. He walked from the park to a church and got in a car with two guys. They drove off and that's where he finally lost me.'

Stijn had no difficulty imagining the smug look on Verbrugge's face.

*

'What did you do then?' Dan asked Stijn. 'The gang couldn't possibly trust you after that.'

'They never trusted me,' Dan. 'You'll have to be patient and wait for the end of the story. I'm here, aren't I? That should comfort you some,' he said with a wink. 'It sure does me.'

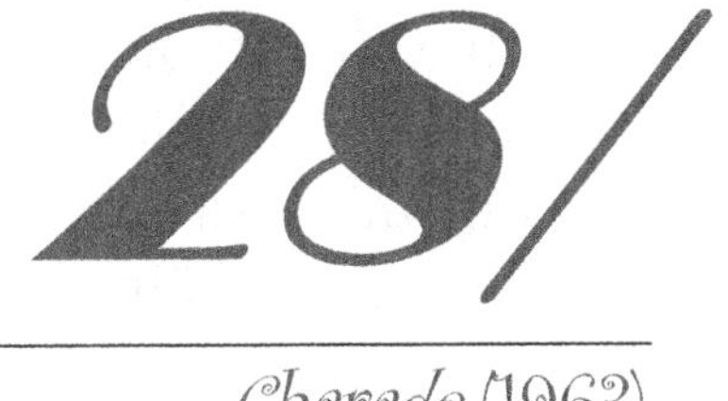

Charade (1963)

Washington, D.C., State Department, Office of the Undersecretary for Middle Eastern Affairs. The 1950s …

'Alice, can you get me the name of that FBI agent who's been asking about a 'Natan Posner?''

'Remind me, boss. Who is 'Posner?''

'Oh, sorry. He was a Dutch Jew who possibly emigrated to Palestine at the end of the war. His case has something to do with that gang of Dutch art thieves the FBI is tracking. 'Posner' is somehow important to their investigation, but I've forgotten the name of the agent working the case.'

*

'Alice' was Alice Townsend, the one indispensable person in the undersecretary's office. Some say Alice was her boss's 'whisperer.' She proudly carried the reputation in the office of being a step or two ahead of his requests.

Undersecretary William 'Bill' Chandler would not take any decision without Alice's participation, even approval. Off and on the past few months, but not for several weeks, Chandler's office had been going through records of the postwar Jewish emigration out of Europe for any trace of 'Natan Posner.'

'Greenleaf,' I believe,' Townsend said without hesitation. 'Let me check again … Yes, Agent Robert Greenleaf.'

'Do we have his number?'

'I've got it right here. Shall I ring him?'

'Please.'

Thirty-seconds later.

'Special Agent Greenleaf.'

'Good morning, Special Agent, this is Bill Chandler at the State Department. I believe you're the person who's interested in the whereabouts of a 'Natan Posner' from Utrecht? The Netherlands?'

In one motion Greenleaf smashed his cigarette in the ash tray on his desk, tilted his chair upright and grabbed his pencil.

'Yes, do you have something for me?'

'I'm afraid not. We've searched every international source we've got for any mention of a 'Posner' who emigrated to Palestine—before 1948—or Israel thereafter. Nothing.'

'Damn!'

'We also found no record of a 'Natan Posner' living in Utrecht or enrolled at the Rotterdam Art Academy. That's the background you asked me to check, right? … Beyond emigration records?'

'Shit! Sorry. Excuse my language. Are you sure? There's a man's life at risk and a sting operation we're running to catch a major art thief. Both are dependent on finding 'Posner.''

'Well, I can't give you a one hundred percent guarantee but it's close to that. We've got nowhere else to look.'

'Will you keep the file active in case something unexpected turns up?'

'Of course, but only as time and resources permit. Before you hang up, there's one more piece of information we need that might aid our search, although it's not about emigration. What names did you say your CI gave for 'Posner's' family?'

'Just a second. Let me look at my notes.'

A minute passed.

'Can I get back to you, Chandler … Wait, hang on. Got em. Thanks, June ...

'The wife is 'Leah,' daughters are 'Klaartje' and 'Maartje'—sounds like twins—and a boy, 'Karel.''

Seconds later.

'Are you sure about those names, Special Agent?'

'Yes, those are what my CI gave me. Got the names right here in my notes, dated the day we debriefed our man on a train in Ohio.'

'But that can't be, Special Agent. Those kids would have *Jewish* names, not Dutch.'

Alice, who stood next to her boss, nodded her agreement and whispers in his ear.

'Are you positive?' Greenleaf said.

'Affirmative. Jews give their children Jewish names. Virtually universal. How much confidence do you have in what your CI has told you?'

'My corroborative sources say confidence in him is 'high.' Everything he told us jibed with independent investigation. The Bureau is very thorough.'

'Special Agent Greenleaf, did you by any chance run those names by a Jewish agent? He'd have told you what I just did. Know what I think? I think your CI made up those names. They're wrong, plus we can't find any of those folks in emigration records. We also checked with the Israelis. No luck there either.'

Alice nodded again.

'So, you're sure about all this? I'm going to discuss it with some of our Jewish agents.'

'I'll offer those same odds as before. Something approaching one hundred percent …

'There's another thing that didn't jibe. It's about the information you gave us on a 'Piet' and a 'Monique

Schoepp.' I'm sorry to say the answer's the same as for 'Posner.' No record that either Schoepp ever lived in Utrecht. That's one hundred percent! I've had my best person corroborate those findings,' he said, smiling at Alice.

Greenleaf threw his head back, stifled another expletive and expelled an audible sigh instead.

'Uh-oh. Hadn't expected that.'

'So, where does that leave your investigation?'

'I'm not sure. Quite possibly it means that white is black or black is white. What you told me a second ago about the Schoepps may be just as important as finding—or not finding—'Natan Posner.' Thanks again, Mr. Chandler.'

'Sure. Anytime. Good luck, Special Agent.'

Alice returned to her desk; more than a hint of satisfaction showed in her face.

*

'Was that true, Stijn?' Dan asked the man across the café table. 'Those people never existed?'

Stijn flushed.

'Ha!' he said, as though Dan trapped him, and he needed to brush off the question. 'You'll have to be patient, Dan, the story doesn't end with one phone call.'

*

When they heard this, Archie and the other listeners—upward of a dozen—grew more impatient with patience.

29/

Suspicion (1941)

Stijn's next move was a private meeting with Verbrugge to discuss the upcoming Frick caper. He wanted to remind 'Teetor,' a name he was loath to utter but couldn't shake, of their earlier conversation about methods of disposing of the paintings safely while scoring a considerable payoff.

Stijn also wanted to get a sense of how much Verbrugge trusted him—or not—particularly after his solo forays into the city and Beeks' clandestine report. Stijn developed a lingering sense, born of those dangerous years of his double life in the Netherlands, that Verbrugge agreed too easily to his solo trip to the Frick. Would a man of his experience trust a reluctant recruit to his pet project so easily? Stijn needed to move forward on the premise that the answer was 'no.' Stijn already suspected someone tailed him that first day in the park.

Stijn suggested that he and Verbrugge go to the park to talk things over, away from the rest of the gang and the women. Verbrugge agreed. Once seated, eerily close to the FBI's signaling bench, Stijn came straight to the point.

'Do you trust me to carry out my part of the plan?'

Stijn's directness took Verbrugge by surprise. He looked away briefly then returned his squinty eyes to Stijn's. Verbrugge may have intended that moment of hesitation to give himself time to think of an answer somewhere between the truth and a lie. Stijn expected the latter.

'Let's just say, 'yes,'' Verbrugge said at last, 'but I'm watching you carefully, De Bruyne. We need your know-how, so, I must trust you.'

Stijn took Verbrugge's reply to mean 'yes' and 'no,' but the gang leader may also have meant 'watching' in the literal sense, which would suggest he did have Stijn followed. What would happen to Stijn when Verbrugge no longer needed his skills?

'Thanks for the vote of confidence,' Stijn said facetiously. 'Understand this, Verbrugge. If you need my knowledge, I must have more free time. I still have work to do at the museum, plus the complicated and delicate job of enlisting buyers.'

Verbrugge hesitated again and frowned.

'We'll see. I'll let you know.'

Then came a stunner.

'I need to walk back to the hotel,' Verbrugge said, 'past that Catholic church … What's the name? … On the corner of Park and East 84th. I've got business there.'

'Don't know the name,' Stijn lied. 'Isn't that quite a bit out of our way?'

'Was Verbrugge dropping a subtle hint that someone followed me there? Was he trying to be clever in the earnest way crooks sometimes are when they try to gain an advantage over a smarter person?'

'Baumann's girlfriend is Catholic,' Verbrugge explained, 'and since she knew we'd be near the church she asked me to find out what time Masses were celebrated during the week.'

'Touché, Verbrugge! What a lie!'

Stijn knew at that moment that Verbrugge knew that Stijn knew what Verbrugge knew. Still, Stijn decided to play along, to see how far Verbrugge was prepared to take his suspicion of Stijn's treachery.

They arrived at St. Ignatius Loyola, and Verbrugge made a clumsy point of jotting down the schedule of Masses posted outside on a bulletin board.

Verbrugge said nothing the rest of the way back to the Franklin, but Stijn thought he detected a satisfied smile cross his face during those final blocks.

Stijn had two immediate concerns: how to free himself from the gang long enough to warn the FBI of his exposure, and how much time remained before his know-how would be insufficient to keep him alive.

30/

The Fugitive (1993)

The sickening smell of defeat swept through the FBI field office on Federal Plaza. Like the ineradicable stink of a horse barn, it lingered in one's nostrils, stuck to the skin.

Special Agent Robert 'Bob' Greenleaf assembled his theft unit to discuss the possible loss of contact with Stijn De Bruyne. They met under the taciturn scrutiny of President Dwight Eisenhower and J. Edgar Hoover whose portraits hung conspicuously in every field office. Their ominous, two-dimensional presences invariably infused the deliberations and decisions of those mustered below with consequence.

'It may be premature to be concerned,' Greenleaf began the meeting, 'but we haven't heard from De Bruyne in days. Our surveillance teams have been watching Central Park discreetly and report no sign of our man ...

'Yesterday, however, our unit monitoring St. Ignatius described seeing De Bruyne in the company of other men whose identities are unknown ...

'De Bruyne warned me about the ruthlessness of the Dutch gang if that's who those others were. They're bad people, folks. During the war, they worked hand-in-glove with the Nazis to hunt down Jews ...

'Regarding St. Ignatius Loyola, I'm confident De Bruyne would not lead Verbrugge to that rendezvous point deliberately, so we must consider the likelihood that Verbrugge discovered the importance of the church to our surveillance and contact scheme, probably by having De Bruyne followed. Verbrugge doubtless took our man there to let him know that he knew, to put him on notice, to put the fear of God in him ...

'Other thoughts, fellas? We believe these guys carried out robberies across the country, amateurish but dangerous versions of what we dealt with in the Thirties ...

'Based on what De Bruyne, our confidential informant, told us, we believe they're planning a 'Big Score' at the Frick Museum ...

'Where do we go from here? How do we reestablish contact with our CI without raising further suspicion? How do we keep De Bruyne alive, assuming that's what we want? Move in and pull him out? Would that blow our operation? What or who's more important, a CI or the overall mission? …

'Holden, what do you think?'

*

'Holden' was Christopher Holden, a fifteen-year veteran of the Bureau and Greenleaf's partner when the latter worked out of the New York field office. Holden, a Mayflower descendant, plus an impressive line of Connecticut Congregationalists, preferred 'Chris' to 'Christopher.'

Chris's grandmother, Susan, from whom he derived his Mayflower pedigree, had worn her other patriotic membership in the DAR as a badge of inviolable honor. She labored mightily to make sure her grandson understood its symbolism and the corresponding civic and moral responsibilities entailed. That meant, among other stiff requirements insisted on by granny, an education at Phillips Exeter Academy and Yale Divinity. She expected Chris, in turn, to impart those values to his progeny.

The ministry, however, did not suit Chris's personality or interests, but the law did. After a specialization in criminal law at Yale, once he formally abandoned a future in the pulpit, he gravitated to police work. He wanted the best, something he knew would have pleased granny despite its secular outlook and modus operandi. The elite law enforcement unit in the United States at the time was, of course, the FBI.

*

'Bob,' Holden said, 'does Verbrugge dare make a move? He suspects De Bruyne is cooperating with us. I don't think we can pull De Bruyne out. We've got nothing concrete on the gang, no overt act. I think the most important question is, how do we protect our man right up to the theft itself?'

'Verbrugge can't be one-hundred percent sure about De Bruyne,' Greenleaf answered. 'I think De Bruyne's smart enough to realize he's got to convince Verbrugge that what he saw is not what it appeared to be ...

'De Bruyne might say something like this: I ran into some old Dutch friends at the church. Let's just hope De Bruyne's drawn the same conclusion about the church visit as we have; that is, 'Teetor'/Verbrugge is suspicious ...

'Also, another point on the positive side, from everything we've seen to this point Verbrugge doesn't know about the park benches, so not all is lost ...

'Let's see if De Bruyne gets free again and leaves a circle. This time don't slash it. Put an arrow in it, but make sure it's obvious that it's pointing to another bench. Wait and see which bench he chooses. Then, as he walks toward it, one of us will come up behind him and whisper the name of a new rendezvous point ...

'Chris, can you work that out?'

'Sure, boss. Emergency entrance to Mt. Sinai Hospital on Madison ought to do. It's one of our regular surveillance posts and it's not far from the park benches and De Bruyne's hotel.'

'Okay then. That's it. We'll need a couple of shifts at the park and the hospital. The lead agent on each stint will be the one to approach De Bruyne. Let's hope he figures out the arrow ...

'Before we go overboard with protecting our CI, there's something else that troubles me—and it should you as well—about De Bruyne. I've checked with the State Department for evidence of the existence or whereabouts of his alibi witnesses. Here's where things go south ...

'The department assures me those so-called witnesses don't exist and probably never did. Moreover, De Bruyne fabricated the names of the so-called Posner children. I think we'd better go forward cautiously on this one, working under the assumption our CI is not entirely on the level. Okay, that's it, unless anyone has questions ...

'Yeah, Chris? What is it?'

'Bob, I think you're right. The whole thing with this guy stinks to high heaven. Our CI may be playing us. From what you've just said and based on our contact with the CI, I don't trust him. For example, what if he's in on the whole operation to rip off the Frick and is using us to deflect attention from himself. We watch the Verbrugge gang while he pulls off the heist on his own. Something like that.'

'*If* he's on the level, Chris, would a guy who hid Jews from the Nazis in his attic for two years at the peril of his life be a phony and a crook?'

'Bob, I'm just saying we need to be careful with this guy and make sure we cover all the possibilities about this planned theft, okay? This guy De Bruyne may be a sociopath or a psychopath, and those types can be charismatic and persuasive. Maybe he never concealed any Jews!'

'Point taken, Chris.'

Greenleaf, however, did not accept the entirety of Holden's analysis, especially the crack about hiding Jews, and he ended the meeting dismissively.

'Okay, we're agreed that we can't trust De Bruyne. Everyone got that?'

The collective nodded obediently.

'Thanks, Chris. Stick around for a minute, please.'

31/

The Street with No Name (1948)

"Dan," Archie broke into the story-telling, "I don't see how Stijn gets out of that mess with his skin intact. 'Teetor.' There was that name again. 'Teetor' had him dead to rights, and the FBI was dreamin' if it believed Stijn would figure out that new arrow scheme. Then it turned out they couldn't trust Stijn from the beginnin'!"

*

It's 1500 at *Renaissance*, however, and lunch is long over. The commons manager asked Dan and Archie to leave for a few minutes to allow the staff to finish cleaning up.

Other residents had noticed the intensity and concentration of our septuagenarians' conversation. Some of the more curious among them had already moved their chairs over to Dan and Archie's table. Still others stood behind them.

The two at the center of all the fuss shrugged off their dismissal by the hostess, buoyed by a chorus of groans and scattered applause.

Dan was also tired, so he promised to resume the story at breakfast.

*

After most of his audience had finished breakfast the next morning, Dan returned to Stijn's story.

"Stijn decided to confront Verbrugge, have it out with him," Dan told the expanded group the following morning, not bothering to review the story for the benefit of newcomers.

Stijn and Verbrugge walked into the Franklin from St. Ignatius Loyola. Before each headed for his room, Stijn grabbed the boss's arm. He figured there was nothing to lose.

'Look, Verbrugge …'

Stijn refused to use the Dutchman's phony American name.

'That diversion of yours to the church was a farce. Baumann's girlfriend no more needed the Mass schedule than I need a broken arm. Why the skullduggery?'

'Okay, wise guy. I'll tell you why. We coerced your participation in this operation. You haven't been part of my group, except in the Netherlands or of any of our earlier operations, so we don't trust you. Do you think I'd let you out of my sight, not knowing where you'd go and what you'd do?'

'It might surprise you to know, Verbrugge, that I'd do the same thing if I were in your shoes. You had me followed. So what? Did whoever you sent see anything suspicious? They couldn't have. Nothing happened!'

'Then who were those people you met at the church?'

'A couple of men from the Dakota train, staunch Catholics. They knew I was interested in art and told me on the train they'd be in New York that day and suggested I meet them after Mass, which I did, even though my knowledge does not extend to church architecture. But they wanted a familiar face to give them a tour of this remarkable church anyway ...

'So, I'm going to tell you some of what I explained to them … and you are going to listen! I don't want there to be any doubt hanging over me any longer!'

Verbrugge let out a sigh that gave away his impatience. He found Stijn's art history lessons tedious and wearing.

'Is this going to take long?'

'Maybe … Maybe not. But you must trust me and if that takes up a few minutes of your precious time, so be it!'

He surprised himself with that outburst and in a rare moment Verbrugge seemed ready to defer to someone other than himself.

'First, Thijs, the exterior. There are two vertical orders, an upper arched window and below that a three-part horizontal division that give the exterior classical balance and reflect the interior space of three aisles.'

Stijn deliberately tried to bore Verbrugge from the outset. And he didn't stop.

'The original plan for the street front included a pair of towers, but the architect and/or builders abandoned this feature, leaving two copper-capped bases ...

'Located directly beneath a front this pediment are two important reminders: the motto of the Society of Jesus, *Ad Majorem Dei Gloriam* (To the Greater Glory of God), and the Great Seal of the Society, composed of a cross, three nails and the letters 'HIS' (the first three letters of Jesus's name in Greek). These reminders proclaim to passersby that St. Ignatius is a Jesuit Parish.'

'Okay! Okay! Enough. I get it,' Verbrugge shouted.

'No! You're going to hear the rest! It's you who doubted me. Remember?'

Stijn calculated that the more he sounded like an expert, the greater the likelihood Verbrugge would accept his lie. Satisfied he had the leader's attention, at least for a few more minutes, he resumed his 'tour.'

'So, about the interior, which was of greatest interest to those visitors ...

'You're in a hurry, so I can boil it down to this: throughout, the church includes American, European, and

African marbles. The aesthetic effect is of cold, unspoiled beauty. The political message is power ...

'Well, there it is, a shortened version of the tour I gave those guys. Unlike you, however, they had the advantage of experiencing the interior in person ...

'Afterward, they drove me back to their hotel for coffee to discuss what they'd seen. Since their hotel wasn't far from the Franklin, I said I could walk from there. That's it ...

'If you want me to complete my part in this operation, you're going to have to have faith in me when I go to the Frick and when I look for buyers. That search isn't going well.'

'Oh? Why not?'

'Because, as I told you earlier, I'm not familiar enough with the criminal element here. I don't have any connections. That's more your line of work, isn't it? I think you should take responsibility for rounding up potential buyers and let me concentrate on the art.'

In truth, Stijn didn't think Verbrugge would have any more success than him. Finding buyers proved far more complicated and critical than anything related to the actual heist.

'You're probably right,' Verbrugge said after a few seconds, looking Stijn up and down. 'I'm going to give you more latitude, but someone will be watching. So, no funny business. Stay away from anyone who's not part of our group. Understand?'

'Right, but I don't want whoever is watching me to get in my way. I may have to do some things that are necessary but might seem suspicious to an amateur like 'Styles' or one of the others. Agreed?'

'Yeah, yeah,' Verbrugge mumbled grudgingly.

32/

Stakeout (1987)

Nearly a week passed before Verbrugge gave Stijn license to return to the Frick. Stijn detoured through the park as he had the day someone followed him, believing that consistent behavior would lessen the gang's suspicion. He wondered if the FBI knew of the gang's mistrust.

When Stijn got to the bench near the pond he saw the old, slashed circle. There was a second oval, one Stijn did not draw, with an arrow through it, not a slash! Who did it? Some kid? Was the FBI trying to tell him something? Was one of Verbrugge's men toying with him? Stijn sat and struggled to grasp the meaning of the mysterious mark.

He looked around. There wasn't much to go on. A few strollers ambling around the pond. A kid trying to get his motorized sailboat to work. Some swans. Three or four partially occupied benches. That was it.

'The FBI's been using a bench to pass along messages, so it makes sense to me to focus on benches. The arrow may point to one of them and I'll find a signal there,' he reasoned.

Stijn cocked his head back and forth, closing one eye and then the other to line up the arrow with one of the benches. He finally narrowed his search to an unoccupied bench about fifty feet away. He started toward it.

He almost reached his target when a stranger brushed by his left shoulder from behind and whispered, 'Emergency Entrance, Mount Sinai.'

Startled, Stijn paused momentarily to assess the incident and speak to the man. It couldn't have been accidental. The walkway was quite wide. The stranger moved briskly away, not bothering to slow or turn around.

It must be the FBI, he decided, otherwise the man would have turned his head or stopped long enough to offer an apology.

Suddenly remembering the hint offered by the stranger, presumably the reason for the bump, Stijn reached into his pocket for a city map and saw that Mt. Sinai Hospital was several blocks away, too far from the Frick for a destination today. He was sure someone had tailed him.

Stijn made two decisions. One, he would continue to the Frick as planned and two, he'd have to come up with a new subterfuge to escape the gang's suffocating control if he were ever going to get to the hospital. He assumed the FBI would be there whenever he could make it, but it wouldn't be today.

Stijn took his time in each Frick room, mapping routes in and out. He'd done this during his earlier visits, but he needed to stall for time. He guessed the longer the gang delayed in executing the robbery, the better chance the FBI would have to put together a counter strategy. Also, by taking his time, a tactic designed to convince Verbrugge the heist would be complicated, Stijn figured he could finagle even more bogus day trips from his leader.

*

A week passed. Panic still shrouded the FBI field office.

'You're sure he understood you, Chris? The spotter said you brushed right by him in a public place.'

'Yeah, I'm sure. He couldn't miss what I said. I heard him hesitate right after I passed, but he said nothing. If someone did what I did and the other person was confused, they'd have reacted ...

'However, he didn't get to the bench or head for the hospital. My guess is that the hospital was a stretch for him that day. When I got to a place where I could watch him, he was already on his way to the museum. I recommend we not give up on Mt. Sinai.'

'Okay,' Greenleaf said, 'it looks like we have no choice but to retain the hospital stakeout until our man can get there. How are the guys holding up over there, Chris?'

'Well enough. They're pros. It's toughest on the married ones. Should we consider shorter shifts? Like the military? Four hours instead of eight?'

'Yeah, that was a bad call on my part. Set it up and give the fellas my apologies, okay?'

*

'Thijs, I've got three more Frick rooms to evaluate before I'll have a workable entry and escape plan. I don't know how things are progressing with you and the others, but I'll need a couple more weeks to finish up.'

'Keep on with your evaluation at the museum, but I'm considering a major tactical change,' Verbrugge said.

Stijn, who was about to walk away, raised his eyebrows.

'I want you to find out if any of the preferred paintings are going on tour. I'm not sure the Frick does that, but if so, get the dates, destination addresses, find shipping labels, types of wrapping paper—anything and everything having to do with moving those things around.'

'That's asking a lot.'

'I don't care what you think it is. Just get it done!'

If Verbrugge was serious with this new gambit, Stijn sensed the gang was becoming overextended. He held his tongue and moved to another topic. He wanted to put some pressure on Verbrugge.

'What about buyers? How's that going?'

'Progress there,' Verbrugge said. 'I'm close to a definite commitment from some Byelorussian Nazis in South River, New Jersey. They were Jew-hunters like us. Got filthy rich on stolen gold and jewelry. After the war, government agencies conspired to smuggle them and hundreds of Eastern European Nazi collaborators and their money into the country, protecting them from investigation and deportation …

'Sound familiar? It ought to. That's exactly how the United States treated us. Many of these Belarus Nazis were directly involved in the murder of Jews during the war, but the government let them into the country anyway. Why? Of all things, to give advice on how to undermine the Soviet Union. That's what their leader told me. Sheesh! These Americans … Is nothing sacred when it comes to national security?'

Verbrugge continued.

'Besides government protection, the Byelorussians have a sizable community in South River. Even private cemeteries decorated with their 'Nazi' flags and symbols. They have a scary reputation outside the government. No one, and I mean no one, bothers them ...

'So, they will make excellent clients of ours. They'll keep everything hush-hush. Someday … Someday, I bet, the Jersey Mob, led by their kingpin, who lives a so-called respectable life in North Caldwell, is going to clean house in South River. Neither of them, Nazis or the Mob, share nicely.'

Stijn was incredulous at the new direction of the plan and Verbrugge's naïveté about working with mobsters.

'You're out of your mind, Thijs! Those guys are exactly the types I warned about. They'll take your loot and then kill you to send a message to others who might be so foolish. They were fighting the Russians! Who were you fighting? The Dutch Resistance? Ha! I'd look for other buyers if I were you ...

'Can't you find some wealthy Mafioso in Queens or on Long Island? A marginally better choice than those Belarus thugs. The Italian would give you top dollar and let you marry his daughter.'

Verbrugge took a step toward Stijn, his hands clenching into fists.

'You're a lousy comedian, De Bruyne, so do your job and stay out of business. Understand?'

Stijn refused to back down. He issued an ultimatum.

'I'm going back to the Frick tomorrow, Thijs. If you send someone to follow me, you can get yourself another expert. I've got witnesses who will rebut any of your accusations. Come to think of it, who are you to accuse me of collaboration? There's no way you can expose yourself with your background. The feds are probably already closing in on the guys that pulled those earlier jobs you brag about.'

Verbrugge grunted and turned away, slowly unclenching.

Checkmate, Stijn concluded.

33/

To Catch a Thief (1955)

Stijn approached Mt. Sinai Hospital cautiously. He took a circuitous route that included the park and museum, checking over his shoulder repeatedly for any sign of someone tailing him. No one. His threat must have worked. He smiled.

On reaching the emergency driveway, he saw the man from the park coming out of the building toward him, dressed in an orderly's outfit. The man didn't stop, but as he passed Stijn he told him to walk toward the double doors of the emergency room.

'Don't stop, don't look back and don't look around.'

'Do you think you were followed?' Greenleaf asked as he opened the double doors.

'I don't think so. I checked and double-checked, then took an indirect route. Verbrugge is afraid I'll go to the feds. That's a laugh, huh?'

'Well, don't underestimate him. He's a seasoned criminal, both here and in Holland. What news?'

'I think Verbrugge is about to make his move. He claims some Byelorussian buyer in Jersey is interested in the paintings. He told me they're nasty people, but then that's the type that'd be interested in heisted art. Right?'

'Yeah, we know all about them. The Justice Department's Office of Special Investigations has been following their every move ...

'Stijn, it pains me to say this because of what you went through in Holland, but the FBI has been involved in protecting the Byelorussians. Look, as citizens, you and I might like to have all these guys put behind bars. I know I would. Our Director … You know who I mean by 'Director'?'

'No, should I?'

'I suppose not. The 'Director' of the FBI is J. Edgar Hoover. He's got his agents looking everywhere for Communists ...

'Politics being what it is these days, pathetically weak at home and abroad and with anti-Communist fervor constantly stirring up the public—guys like McCarthy, Nixon and that so-called Un-American congressional committee—the government is afraid to take any action against people who profess to hate Communists no matter the crimes they've committed. That's the Byelorussians in spades. Our operation is quite low on Hoover's to do list.

No Commies, just ordinary thieves. Sad situation, don't you think? …

'Never mind. What else do you have for us?'

'Well, something rather important, I think. Verbrugge made an interesting request. Said he's considering a 'tactical change' in plan. Wants me to gather all the information I can about any art that's leaving the museum—going on tour or on loan to another gallery or museum. He wants destination addresses, duplicate shipping labels, types of wrapping paper and crates.'

Greenleaf paused.

'That makes sense. Easier and safer to divert the stuff enroute than break into the museum. We've dealt with this kind of theft before. If he decides to go that way, we'd know the exact time to close in ...

'Moving that stuff would be very public. Advantage us. On the other hand, with a break-in it's a crap shoot, but that's where you come in. We're counting on you to let us know exactly how and when they plan to make their move, if that's what it's to be ...

'Are they well-armed? Revolvers, Tommy-guns, rifles, shotguns, grenades, dynamite? Any gas masks?'

'Not sure about their arsenal. I've only seen Verbrugge's pistol, which he pointed at me in Ennis. No gas masks that I'm aware of.'

'Okay, that's something else you need to work on. We don't want to walk into a situation where we're outgunned. The Bureau experienced enough of that in the Thirties with bootleggers, bank robbers and racketeers ...

'Tell me about the other gang members. Do you think they're as committed as Verbrugge to a life of crime?'

'Absolutely not. I've never been impressed with any of them, their intelligence or anything else. Verbrugge has hold over them, just as he thinks he does with me. He's Svengali-like ... Charismatic. As close to a psychopath or sociopath as anyone I've ever known. He preys on people's weaknesses.'

Greenleaf winced, recalling Chris Holden's corresponding estimation of Stijn.

'I've never seen any of them stand up to him,' Stijn continued, 'but if one does balk, as I have, he'll back down. At root, he's a coward. If you corner him and he sees no way out, he'll give up. Too cowardly to kill himself. I think he'll look at surrender as a new challenge. 'How can I manipulate these guys?' he'd wonder. That sort of attitude.'

'Wow! You must have studied psychology. That's quite a breakdown. All useful information. It's true, most criminals are just as you describe. Cowards ...

'It's time we let you get back to your assignment. Chris Holden, the man who met you in the park, will be your handler from here on. Since the verbal technique of contacting you worked so well, we'll continue that. Just go about your routine, but should you have more information, leave your circle on the second bench and look for an arrow. If you walk in the direction shown, Chris will find you. Got it?'

'Yes.'

*

This time Stijn got no grief from Verbrugge about his absence. His threat to quit the project apparently succeeded. If the gang had followed him this time, he'd be dead. But he still needed answers to the FBI's questions about the gang's preparation, so he came straight to the point.

'Thijs, will you be armed if you go into the museum?'

'Of course!'

34/

Manic Cop (1988)

The mysterious blonde, whose arrival at the café hours before had briefly supplanted Stijn's infatuation with the host. She set down her coffee cup, rose from her booth and instead of going to the cashier and the door, as customers normally would, she turned toward our table under the watchful eye of the host.

Stijn, who had been leaning forward while recounting his story, turned and marked her movement carefully. Then, wincing noticeably, he slumped back in his seat.

'That's odd,' I thought. 'I hadn't noticed any discomfort on his part earlier. But with the blonde headed toward us, he seemed either content, as though someone had lifted a huge weight from his shoulders, or he wasn't content and that weight hadn't been lifted.'

The blonde stopped next to our table, her face empty of expression.

Stijn looked up, wincing again. He started to rise, trying to be courteous, but she stopped him with a hand on his shoulder.

'Don't bother,' she said calmly, her face still masking whatever emotion she felt.

With the other hand, she flipped open her credentials and, just as smartly, snapped the leather folder shut and returned it to her hip pocket. From what I could see in that brief instant the folder appeared much like the one Stijn described as belonging to Agent Borst. But I was wrong.

'Highway Patrol,' she said authoritatively. 'Stijn De Bruyne, based on an APB we received from the FBI, I have a warrant for your arrest for the theft of valuable paintings from the Frick Museum in New York City. Do you wish to see the warrant?'

Stijn said nothing. I tried to make myself small.

My first thought was, the FBI had double-crossed him. Instead of him working with the Bureau to nail the Verbrugge gang, they put the onus for the theft on him! Why would they do that? I had no answer.

'In addition, the Justice Department's Office of Special Investigations is considering other charges regarding to your wartime activities in Holland,' she droned on matter-of-factly.

Stijn stayed perfectly still, staring straight ahead.

'You have the right to remain silent. Anything you say can and will be used against you in a court of law.

You have the right to an attorney. If you cannot afford an attorney, one will be appointed for you. Do you understand these rights as I have stated them?'

Stijn just sat there for a few seconds, not returning her gaze, not moving, not showing any emotion. Finally, looking not to her but to me, he spoke.

'Well, well, well. Hello, Brooke.'

My companion treated the blonde derisively, paying no attention her question about his constitutional rights or the mention of Holland.

'How did you find me?'

'The APB. Put two and two together.'

She turned to me.

'All-Points-Bulletin,' she said in a manner that reminded me of one of my grammar-school teachers. Very patronizing.

'You seemed familiar when you came in,' Stijn said, returning to their duel. 'Been trying to place you all afternoon. The braid through me off, though. Like it. You didn't have it before. Nobody could guess who you work for.'

He paused briefly, trying to judge her reaction to his slights.

'Dan,' Stijn said a moment later, obviously trying to get her goat, 'meet Sergeant Ebbet Brooke Dunlap. Sweetness itself, isn't she? How long have you been a cop, Brooke?'

'Ten plus,' she answered nonchalantly, without expression.

'Quite a handle, huh, Dan?'

Stijn was addressing me, but his eyes, suddenly narrowed and cold, never left hers. He tried to make the comment about her name sound pleasant, but it didn't.

Across the room, the host continued to chat with other patrons but maintained an interest in our table.

*

Ebbet Brooke Dunlap hailed from Riverton, Wyoming, where she grew up with two brothers, Tim and Warren. Sergeant Tim Dunlap died near Bastogne during the 'Bulge.' Corporal Warren Dunlap, a deadly BAR gunner, returned home with the Silver Star and the nightmares that came with it.

Both young men belonged to the Riverton Police Department before their enlistments and, as part of her desire to honor their service, Brooke determined to carry on the family tradition. She received an associate's degree in criminal justice from Eastern Wyoming College in Torrington and joined the highway patrol.

She and Stijn met at a post-game party in Torrington following one of the college's football victories. Stijn was on his way to the Wind River, having just finished some landscapes in Nebraska.

*

"I realized Stijn's demeanor and tone changed because of the manner in which he spoke to Officer Dunlap. He was someone I didn't know … or want to know. I was shocked ...

"Stijn, however, couldn't let it go. I think he was trying to humiliate Sergeant Dunlap because she seemed to have the advantage."

*

'Dan,' Stijn pressed on, 'her father named her 'Brooke' after the 'Brooklyn' Dodgers baseball club and 'Ebbet' after their ball park.

Stijn's eyes never left hers.

''Ebbet' never caught on with Brooke,' Stijn said, winking at her, 'but I suppose it gave daddy no end of satisfaction.'

Stijn's caustic remark failed to unnerve the officer. She listened patiently, offering no visible reaction, then continued with her job.

'Stand up, please, Mr. De Bruyne.'

Her formality was telling. That and her patience surprised me considering the circumstance and Stijn's condescending manner.

Stijn rose slowly, pushing himself up with the help of the tabletop, wincing noticeably again, tossing his head slightly back.

'Turn around and place your hands behind your 
back.'

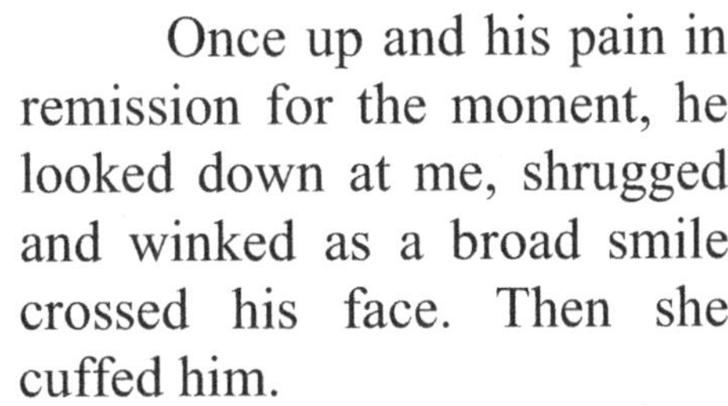
Once up and his pain in remission for the moment, he looked down at me, shrugged and winked as a broad smile crossed his face. Then she cuffed him.

I thought I was watching a movie!

'Better be careful who you associate with,' Dunlap said sternly, looking straight at me. 'You look like a man who ought to know better than this,' she said, nodding toward her prisoner.

Then she turned him gently by the arm and marched him out of the café. Like she owned the place. At that moment, I believed she did.

The vigilant host had stopped in her tracks and followed the pair with her eyes until the door closed behind them. Funny about her. I thought she looked stunned, as though De Bruyne was someone she knew beyond his being a customer.

I never laid eyes on Stijn De Bruyne again … in person, at least. That's where his story ended ... Maybe.

35/

The Getaway (1992)

Stijn's arrest grabbed the headline in the local paper the following day. You couldn't expect the highway patrol to make an arrest in a small-town café and then perp-walk the prisoner out of the place without notice. The article said that Stijn De Bruyne pleaded *nolo contendere* to all charges presented by the district attorney at his arraignment.

*

Several months later and a week after his conviction in a bench trial, Stijn De Bruyne, still handcuffed to a hospital bed, died of acute pancreatic cancer as he awaited extradition to the International Criminal Court in The Hague.

Reading about Stijn's humiliating passing, I felt completely empty. My life seemed to have ended as well. I had invested a lot in his story.

Was there any truth, even a sliver of it, to the story he told me? Probably not. Still, I wanted—I needed—a definitive answer, but I realized that not even the FBI knew the truth or falsity of it. But they shared some of their theories about the case after the Bureau transferred the agents you already know to desk jobs. It turned out I knew one of the Special Agents newly assigned to the case. He's the son of one of my buddies back in Columbus, Nebraska.

He may not have told me everything the Bureau had, but he felt okay revealing what follows.

*

Another art heist took place in San Francisco about six months after Stijn died. I just happened to have my TV on that night. The news anchor explaining the story needed to fill time in the broadcast, so she dredged up the Frick case, calling it a prototype for the San Francisco job. I can't say if that's true or not, but the broadcast was interesting for another reason.

It showed grainy stills and dimly lit, black and white film of Stijn—TV was primitive then—and a man I thought to be Wiktor Stankievich—I couldn't see his face clearly—a Byelorussian big shot from Jersey who, because of his association with Stijn and his illegal entry into the United States in the late 1940s, faced his own immigration and war crimes charges and, of course, theft of the Frick paintings. Stankievich was Stijn's 'collector,' I gathered.

What the reporter said next floored me! Blindsided me! She alleged my friend—I'm sure he wouldn't mind my calling him 'friend'—was the real mastermind behind the Frick job and those earlier strong-arm holdups, presumably Verbrugge's. Stijn, she concluded with dramatic flair, was also a renowned and much-despised Jew hunter in Holland during the war!

That second revelation stunned me a second time, and I wrestled with the realization that everything Stijn De Bruyne told me was a lie. Still can't figure out how I misjudged him. Kinda makes you leery of making friends with anyone.

"Maybe you folks noticed that about me," Dan said, turning to his *Renaissance* audience. "I never did talk much until now."

*

"What happened to the gang, Dan?" a dumbfounded Archie asked. "Did they get caught?"

In a sense, they did. Years later. The case broke wide open when De Coster's girlfriend, Allison Brown, ratted on them. Spilled the beans.

The FBI had enlisted a New York City plainclothes officer, Elizabeth Spencer, to keep an eye on Brown. Spencer eventually began a casual conversation with Brown at a donut bar. They discussed the weather, New York manners and other trivial stuff, all the while Spencer pretended to be a curious out-of-towner interested in the big city. Over a period of a few weeks Spencer became Brown's friend and confidant.

It turned out that De Coster was a brutal misogynist and, under steady, gentle pressure from Spencer it didn't take long for Allison to break down and reveal the entire plan in an act of revenge against her boyfriend. As they say, she sang like a canary!

De Coster, a weak sycophant of Verbrugge, followed suit under intense FBI interrogation.

But—and here's biggest doozy of them all—those two, De Coster and Brown, had nothing to do with the robbery itself! Nor did Beeks, Baumann or De Bruyne. Brown and De Coster lied to the cops simply put a stop to the questioning and bad food. Their FBI interrogators, of course, the ones the Bureau demoted, believed they had cracked the case.

"Then who did pull off the job? I assume there was a robbery?" one of Dan's listeners asked.

"There was indeed!"

36/

How to Steal a Million (1966)

Three minutes past midnight on precisely the Sunday Verbrugge had selected for the heist, a car—could have been a '53 Ford; no one's sure—pulled up to the side entrance of the Frick Museum. A man in a police uniform waited for about an hour in the car, trying to calm his nerves with cigarettes or just making sure the FBI was not lying-in wait. Then he slipped on a rubber head mask.

At 0100, give or take a couple of minutes, a Frick security guard returned to the security desk from his rounds. He was the only person in the building.

For some reason—the guard couldn't explain convincingly, or he didn't want to explain convincingly, and the cops couldn't figure it out—he opened and quickly shut the outside door, claiming he did it to make sure it was locked. An intentional signal? Part of his training, he said.

He told the cops later that the security logs would show he tested the door on other nights as well. The FBI seized the logs but has declined to comment on what they showed.

Twenty-five minutes later the uniformed man outside set down an oversize shoulder bag where no one could see it from the lobby. It held a small flashlight, wire cutter, gloves, and glass cutter. He pressed the buzzer near the door.

When he was sure the sound had alerted the guard, he yelled, 'Police! Your security alarm went off. The door, remember? Let me in!'

The guard knew he should not open for an uninvited guest, but he was unsure if the rule applied to police officers.

There he stood, the guard said later, one of New York's finest, waving at me through the glass. Hat, coat, badge—he looked like a cop.

It seems Verbrugge's 'girls' had done their job well.

The guard decided to buzz him in.

The intruder went straight to the security desk where the anxious guard waited.

'You look familiar,' he said to the guard. 'I have a warrant on you.'

That left the guard dumbfounded and unable, as per his training, to deal with what followed.

The 'cop' drew a .38 revolver, deliberately altered to look like a genuine service piece.

'Step away from the desk and place your hands behind your head,' he ordered.

The guard stepped from behind his desk where he had access to the only alarm button in the museum. Intentional? No one's sure.

'Hey, man. I've got a family … kids. Just do what you need and leave. I swear I won't rat on you,' the guard whimpered.

The 'police officer' then asked for the guard's identity card, ordered him to stand facing the wall, and handcuffed him.

'Why are you arresting me?' he said. 'You couldn't possibly have a warrant on me!'

'Shut up! I'm not arresting you. This is a robbery, fool. Don't give me any problems and you won't get hurt.'

'You going to shoot me in the back?' the guard cried. 'Please, mister.'

The thief ignored the man's pleading, went back to the door, and put a pencil on the threshold against the jam, letting the door settle back gently. To anyone outside, the door would appear to be closed.

The thief then prodded the guard down to the basement, handcuffed him to some water or heating pipes, and wrapped duct tape around his hands, feet, and head, leaving breathing holes.

The guard had decided by this time he wasn't going to die.

The thief returned to the main floor. He put on the gloves and hurried down the hallway to the Vermeer, his flashlight's dome of light bouncing on the floor and walls in keeping with his pace. Standing before the painting and putting the flashlight between his teeth, he used the wire cutter and his strength to cut and yank *Officer and Laughing Girl* from the wall.

In doing so, he dropped the wire cutter and the flashlight reflexively fell out of his mouth. Somehow, he managed to catch both in one hand before they got below his waist, while still holding the Vermeer with the other hand. Beads of perspiration burst through the skin on his brow. He stuffed the Vermeer into the bag.

Next, he moved swiftly through the remaining hallways and galleries and, using the same technique as he had with the Vermeer, retrieved the Monet, the Piero and the Van Eyck from their premiere gallery locations. Twice he nearly dropped the Monet and Van Eyck; he had underestimated the size and bulk of both. He added them to the bulging bag.

Only twenty minutes had passed since he left the guard in the basement. He set down the bag of paintings and tools behind the security desk and quickly returned to the basement.

Fearful that now he might die, the guard squirmed and tried to speak. His red, watery eyes bulged.

'The morning shift will free you when they arrive. Sorry for the inconvenience. Nice doing business with you.'

With that, he left the same way he came in. No one saw him or heard from him again.

*

Oh, yes. Special Agents Greenleaf, Holden, Borst and Freeman? They were nowhere near the Frick that night. Their CI, confidential informant—Stijn—had failed them. And where was Stijn that night? Only two people knew.

37/

The Wizard of Oz (1939)

"Do you recall my mention of a Byelorussian collector, the guy I've called 'Stankievich?'" Dan asked his expanding *Renaissance* audience.

"Well, he wasn't simply the collector. He had been De Bruyne's *partner* from the moment the gang arrived in New York."

Dan's audience uttered a collective gasp.

The thief intended the paintings for *Stijn*, not Stankievich. The person who called himself 'Stankievich' was probably not Stankievich at all but some anonymous Belarus guy, a fall guy for some bigshot. But he was a necessary element in the plan to throw suspicion away from Stijn. Our Dutchman must have paid him handsomely. Anyway, at that point we do know the paintings wound up in Wiktor Stankievich's hands.

"Was he the thief? How did Stijn get away?"

Dan avoided the question about the thief but explained instead how Stijn escaped the gang.

It was quite easy. Before the gang knew what was up, Stijn gave everyone the slip, including the FBI, and vamoosed out of the city for points west, to Wyoming, it's thought.

'Stankievich' was supposed to deliver the originals to Stijn at the secret western location. It was somewhere near where I met him that day in the café. But here's the shocker! No one knows whether Stijn or the paintings ever made their way to the chosen destination. They simply vanished.

*

Then things got nasty. Months after the heist, the feds, acting on an anonymous tip, found 'Stankievich,' his head, arms and legs severed, all of it stuffed into a 55-gallon burn barrel in a toxic dump in South River, New Jersey. Bullet holes riddled his torso. An entry wound right between his eyes suggested a Mob hit.

Someone, presumably the assassin, pinned a blood-stained note to Stankievich's torso just below the neckline. It amounted to a bastardization of John Wilkes Boothe's shouted explanation for his having just shot Abraham Lincoln: 'Thus to Commies and Tradors.'

"So, maybe the paintings and Stankievich never left Jersey. Probably some local Don in Jersey who can't spell has the paintings," Dan said with a chuckle. "But let me continue. The story gets stranger and stranger."

When the FBI ran the fingerprints of the man in the barrel, they discovered they belonged to?

Dan waited for his listeners to supply a name. But they all looked at each other with puzzled expressions.

"No guesses?" Dan asked again.

A wag standing on the perimeter of the group said meekly, "Jimmy Hoffa"? That brought down the roof!

Once the laugher died down Dan confessed: "*Theo Vandermoelen*! You remember, the former head of Utrecht's *NSB*, who was currently under an arrest warrant issued by the International Criminal Court to answer for war crimes. It's supposed he managed to slip away when the Allies closed in, probably the same way Verbrugge's gang, including Stijn, avoided capture by the Allies, authorities guessed."

"Wow!" Archie exclaimed.

"Yeah," Dan replied. "Quite a development, huh ...?

"The Bureau concluded the Mob killed 'Vandermoelen/Stankievich' over a heroin or cocaine deal gone sour soon after he returned from the West … or before he even left. Those Jersey Italians were just itching to get over on the Byelorussians. Couldn't stand them anywhere near their turf, plus the fact the Italians believed they were Commies! The Mob had no idea they were dealing with a Dutch fascist, not a Byelorussian."

*

Dan rolled out more surprises.

"Archie, I learned there may have been a house on Linnaeuslaan or some other street in Utrecht, but there were never any Posners or Schoepps …

"I used to wonder what happened to Marge Balfour and those plans she and Stijn hatched. I asked myself many times if she were imaginary. Another of the many lies Stijn spun. Fits the old maxim that once you tell a lie you must keep lying to hide the first one ...

"Shoot, come to think of it there may never have been a 'Stijn De Bruyne' as I've described him! We have only his word for any of this. Do you trust that?"

"No! Certainly not," Archie agreed. "And do you wanna hear what else I think? I think Stijn was Verbrugge! Or vice versa. Doesn't matter, really. And if that's so, was Stijn the brutish street thug that he described to you or a lover and storyteller with a penchant for lyin'?"

"Maybe both," Dan said, shrugging. "Probably both."

From behind Archie a woman called out.

"Why go to those lengths? Pretending to hide Jews? Pretending to collaborate with the Nazis? Pretending to help the FBI? Making up a gang that never existed? Everything he told you, Dan, was a lie! Why?"

"Nora ... May I call you Nora?"

"Yes, of course."

"I've thought about all that, and the only conclusion I've come to is that he just loved telling stories ... and lying! Simple as that sounds. Gave him control over people. Part of his pathology. Remember, he said he'd loved doing it since childhood."

"Nah, he was a sociopath!" another resident blurted out. "No moral compass. Didn't give a rat's ass about anyone. Total manipulator …

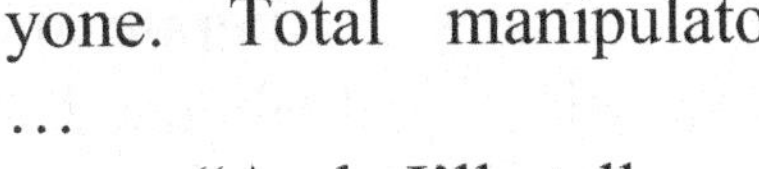

"And I'll tell you what else I think. Yes, De Bruyne was Verbrugge, but the gang was real, the only difference being that Stijn was its leader. 'Verbrugge' was just a fiction created to give De Bruyne cover from the law and from you, Dan."

Others nodded their agreement.

"Well, you gotta admit don't you, Arch," Dan continued, "morality, persona, and lying aside, the whole cockamamie story *is* still fascinating, right? A darn good yarn and a lingering mystery. *But*—and this is a big but—none of us or anyone else ought to believe a word of it. Seems clear most of us don't."

Everyone is quiet for a few moments, digesting the unfolding revelations.

Dan looked briefly toward the windows in front of the pool before turning back to his larger audience.

"Well, maybe he was a sociopath, but I can't help thinking Stijn just enjoyed telling a story and watching people swallow it! Heck, maybe that's what I've been doing. Anyway, I bet Stijn's having a good chuckle 'up there.'"

Everyone but Dan looked up in unison. Learned behavior.

"Truth may never be the ultimate measure of a story or of a man … or a woman."

Dan's deliberate mention of a woman, when the discussion had focused entirely on Stijn De Bruyne, seemed out of place but went unnoticed.

"I dunno. Maybe it is ... It should be, I think," Archie said.

His conclusion satisfied everyone ... almost.

"Dan," a man in a wheelchair spoke for the first time, "something you've told us is really bothering me, but no one has mentioned it. How is it that Stijn could describe the robbery to you in such detail when he left town beforehand?"

Others looked at each other and nodded their agreement.

Dan smiled and shrugged. He was caught. His story had backfired. 'Hoist on his own petard,' so to speak. He had no answer, so, he equivocated.

"Well, Harry, I suppose we'll have to rely on our imaginations to answer that. I have my opinion, and I'll bet it's not much different than yours.

Everyone in the group nodded, suggesting they had an answer as well.

"But it seems to me there's a broader point," Dan continued. "It's unlikely that either mental imagery or reality will suffice when trying to make sense of the character and behavior of 'Stijn De Bruyne.' He was too much the chameleon, too much the master of impersonation and deflection: an artist, a thief, and a liar. All very human, doncha think? That's the point, it seems to me."

38/

The Woman in the Window (1944)

Fifteen minutes later calm had returned to the commons dining room. That quarter hour had given Dan's audience a necessary break from the exhausting story, a break that included more coffee and even more bathroom trips.

Gradually, a larger group of residents reassembled around Dan and Archie's table, arms folded, or the gents' hands clasped between legs, or, in the case of the ladies, at rest in their laps. They all engaged in small talk, waiting on Dan, prepared, they thought, for more surprises from the 'Giants man.'

As if on cue, after everyone had returned and settled into the seats they had just left, Dan Wiley removed his cap and rubbed his forehead. After he had returned the cap and adjusted the angle just right, his eyes began to twinkle and a broad, impish smile crossed his face.

He sat relaxed in his chair, thinking before speaking. He was aware of the impact of his revelation about Stankievich's true role and identity, and he wanted to them to think about that as he prepared them for another surprise.

He'd adroitly avoided the question about the robber's identity, he thought.

His listeners—there were now more than two dozen residents and staff, including Archie's fetching waitress—sensed the change in their storyteller's demeanor. The twinkle in his eye was a dead giveaway; he had something more to say and was dying to spill it.

"Come on, Dan," someone finally broke the silence There's much more, isn't there? Damn well better be after all this!"

"All right, if you insist," Dan teased, as though he was reluctant to continue.

"Come on, Dan!" another impatient listener shouted.

"Okay, but just remember, you asked for it!"

He paused again, arms folded, trying to intensify the anticipation of his listeners.

"Take a look at the woman by the windows, but don't be too obvious about it," he said, gently nodding and pointing with the index finger of one folded arm toward the windows overlooking the pool and shuffleboard courts.

Some slowly turned their heads. Some merely shifted their eyes.

The woman who sat alone under those windows seemed suddenly alert to the room gone silent. That, or she'd seen the stares. But she didn't return the interest of Dan's listeners.

"Okay, all of you know the person I mean. But think of *how* we know her. She's the one who's always fashionably dressed, not that you ladies aren't ... at times."

Laughter.

"She's the one among you who wears an abundance of expensive jewelry that ought to be locked up but isn't. It's odd. On one hand she wants attention, but on the other, not."

Dan waited a moment to let that soak in. Then, as if to reinforce his point …

"Any of you ever join her?"

The audience looked to each other, but no one spoke up. Several people shook their heads.

"So, it's agreed. She sits mostly alone. She's also one of a handful of people in this room who're *not* listening to the story. Not even looking our way."

Dan's followers turned their heads as one toward the windows, their curiosity swelling.

"There's an aura of mystery about her, don't you think?" Dan continued. "To my knowledge no one's ever said where her money comes from or how much there is. Yet people talk a lot about money here ...

"Think about it, folks. She's gone most of the year, not just the hot months. Then, one day, unexpectedly, there she is, back at that table. I've heard she travels all over the world and donates handsomely to charities. If she weren't so classy looking, you'd say she's 'filthy rich.'"

Some chuckling.

"Well, maybe she is."

Dan wanted that to sink in. He hoped someone would blurt out the story's dénouement.

But the audience only nodded, again in unison, shifting their eyes from Dan to the lady and back again without being too obvious, unsure of the direction the story had taken with this new focus on the mysterious woman. They waited and hoped for more.

Dan milked their anticipation for what seemed to many an eternity but was no more than a half minute.

"Maybe," he resumed, "maybe there's no mystery about her at all," he repeated, again with that mischievous twinkle in his eye.

His seated listeners scooched toward the edge of their chairs.

"Careful, Alice," someone warned just before Alice's chair was ready to collapse and dump her unceremoniously on her derrière.

"Ever notice *how* she sits at that table, even when she shares it? She always faces the wall holding several paintings."

He waited for people to glance at the wall; some did as though they'd never seen it before.

"She seems wholly uninterested in what people outside are doing at the shuffleboard courts or the swimming pool. Have you ever looked closely at those paintings?"

Most of Dan's audience shook their heads.

"If you have, you would've noticed they're western landscapes."

Dan paused, allowing one more bombshell clue to sink in. His audience murmured among themselves. Some gasped. They were thinking about the woman and those paintings, but no one saw what came next.

Dan's demeanor changed.

"Beth?" Dan continued, looking to Archie's fetching waitress who stood at the rear of the group, which had huddled even more tightly around Dan and Archie's table.

Beth smiled appreciatively at his mention of her name. Archie beamed.

"It's your moment, Beth. Tell the folks about the mystery lady."

"Oh, I don't think there's any mystery a'tall about *her*, Dan," she said on cue, in a manner she apparently believed consistent with Dan's melodramatic finale. "She's Mrs. Marge Balfour. Great tipper!'

Many of the listeners gasped loudly. It was as though someone had suddenly drained the room of all its air ... a collective sucking gasp … a balloon gone limp.

39/

The Big Sleep (1946)

pecial Agents Frank Borst, Robert Greenleaf, Charles Freeman and Christopher Holden had flunked J. Edgar Hoover's charge:

'Do Not Fail'

All four lost their seniority over the Frick fiasco. Before forced retirement, each spent two decades speaking before audiences at civic and service organizations across the country: Rotarians, Kiwanians, Lions … the Boy Scouts. Even in front of inattentive school kids happy to be out of class and sitting as a general assembly—regardless of the topic and presenter.

With charts and occasional testimony from former communists and in keeping with Director Hoover's obsession, the demoted agents explained the critical role of the Bureau in saving the country from communism. No one, however, thought to ask them about catching ordinary thieves, nor did the agents mention such seemingly mundane Bureau activities. Christopher Holden's granny must have been spinning in her grave!

*

Marge Balfour passed away at *Renaissance* four years after Dan wrapped up Stijn De Bruyne's story. and two years before Dan Wiley and Archie McIntyre.

After the heady days of 'Stijn's Story,' she never again sat alone overlooking the shuffleboard courts and swimming pool or, for that matter, anywhere else at *Renaissance.* Other residents suddenly found her gregarious and good company, but Marge Balfour never, ever talked about Stijn, the robbery, the paintings, or the source of her money. Not to a single soul ... or so legend has it.

We could guess, of course, that Marge knew of Stijn's plan to steal the paintings and took possession of them from 'Stankievich' while waiting for her lover to arrive from New York. Stijn and Marge's lifestyle preceding his demise suggests they sold the paintings—buyer or buyers unknown—for a tidy sum. No one, it seems, ever knew of Marge Balfour's role in the scheme ... or so legend has it.

*

Of course, we could also hypothesize about Marge Balfour's direct involvement, but there is no need.

Finally, Dan Wiley told his listeners of frequent conversations with Marge Balfour. Up to that moment, apparently, no one had ever noticed. What did they discuss? He told her everything Stijn had said to him, and she confirmed events having to do with that part of Stijn's life they shared, including her accessory role in the Frick theft.

'I do think I understand Stijn De Bruyne,' Dan had said to Marge one afternoon. 'He was an artist, a thief and a crass liar. Everything you are not.'

He didn't mention, of course, the distinct possibility that she was everything that Stijn was.

'On top of that,' he continued, 'maybe he was also a sociopath.'

'Probably all those things, Dan,' she said, not batting an eye.

Dan, puzzled, paused a moment to assess her ready agreement to his assertions.

'Then here's my question, Mrs. Balfour,' he said after recomposing himself, 'something that's been giving me fits ever since I met Stijn De Bruyne, a concern you apparently share ...

'If you agree with my description of his character and behavior, as you say you do, why did you help with his scheme? You were taking an awful chance. They might have caught you or something much worse. After all, there were those Byelorussians!'

'The answers are easy, Dan. I *don't* disagree with your assessment of Stijn at all. But I *loved* him. He *was* charismatic—maybe a sociopath—irresistible and very charming … good to me. As for the Byelorussians, 'ignorance is bliss.' I never knew of their involvement or any danger they represented. It's as simple as that. I didn't mind the money, either!' she added with a delicious smile.

*

"I couldn't think of another thing to ask her," Dan confessed to his listeners.

"I had no training as a reporter, so, I probably missed opportunities to press her further. But how far should you go in challenging an elderly woman in love with her memories? How much invasion of her privacy would be reasonable? Perhaps I'd already gone too far. She's only going to tell you things that will protect her and her memories, true or not. So, I left it there."

*

Having reached the end of her life, and in a will unsealed a year after her death, Marge Balfour bequeathed what was left of of her riches to Archie's fetching waitress, Elizabeth 'Beth' Jordan, her only friend and confidant on the *Renaissance* staff. A 'great tipper,' indeed!

*

Beth Jordan left *Renaissanc*e, enrolled at State University and earned a degree in English. Her quest for self-improvement didn't end there, however. Jordan became a successful mystery writer.

Although Beth created another life for herself, her heart still belonged to *Renaissance* … and a special resident. With her bequest from Marge, the money she made from her writing plus the tips she saved—mostly from Marge—she returned 'home' and bought *Renaissance*!

Then, of all things, Beth Jordan, elevated from 'fetching waitress' to fetching owner, up and married Archie McIntyre! The mischievous smile and the faded tam-o'-shanter had finally worked their hoped-for magic.

Dan was wrong. A persistent old man *can* turn a beautiful woman's head. Beth made Archie the happiest man in Arizona for the entirety of the two years before his death. She was sure Marge would approve.

*

Try as the FBI might in the matter of the Frick, and it had tried hard, the Bureau never made a case against anyone except the man whose identity was unknown but went by 'Stijn De Bruyne.' Let's just say the robbery made some people very rich … or dead.

The Bureau, however, didn't come away empty handed from its failed investigation. A year after Marge Balfour's death, agents received another anonymous tip—it seems always so—in a crudely written letter, coincidentally dated about the time of Marge's passing but only recently mailed.

The letter directed agents to a South River, New Jersey, garage where they found the missing Frick property, covered by waterproof tarps, dust and cobwebs. The decrepit wooden structure, otherwise empty, its door with broken windows unhinged and falling away, had no listed owner or renter. How the four paintings got there, and who tipped the FBI is a mystery ... or so legend has it.

The Van Eyck, Piero, Monet, and Vermeer, said to have received no visible damage after restorers finished their meticulous examination, again graced the gallery walls of the Frick Museum. Curators, benefactors, and docents at the tycoon's former home on 5th Avenue denied any paintings ever went missing, despite patrons' claims to the contrary.

*

A few retired lawyers and other residents who heard 'Stijn's Story' filed a succession of Freedom of Information requests with the FBI about Verbrugge and the other gang members. To each, the reply came back the same:

> The Bureau was unable find documents relating to the following: 'Thijs Verbrugge,' 'Peter De Coster,' 'Joost Beeks,' 'Martijn Baumann' and 'Jeroen Pieters.'

Nonetheless, a surviving witness kept 'Stijn's Story' alive and a *Renaissance* legend.

'You can be sure it's all true,' the proud guardian of the story insisted to residents, 'every word of it. I wrote it all down, word for word, the first time Dan Wiley told it to my husband.'

*

Archie McIntyre's widow, his one-time fetching waitress and the memorialist of 'Stijn's Story,' eventually sold *Renaissance* and moved to Midland, Texas, with her new husband, a wealthy oil man. Those who knew the story of the thieving, lying Dutch artist wondered what would become of the tale without Beth. They needn't have worried.

The highest (winning) offer for the property came from a tall middle-aged man with a slight accent that no one at *Renaissance* could place. He immodestly professed himself an art connoisseur whose small fortune, he bragged to Beth and the mortgage lender, came mostly from places where the preferred game of chance was 'Texas Hold 'em.' He signed the real estate papers as 'Karel Posner' of South River, New Jersey.

No one, including Beth, who was eager to get on with her new life, took notice of these stunning clues—the game, the name, and the place—or bothered to ask what advantage Posner, clearly a man of estimable poker skill, saw as an advantage in settling into the ownership of an 'old folks' facility.

Nonetheless, the new owner adapted more quickly than one could reasonably expect of a person with little or no experience in managing a retirement complex. Soon, new generations of residents spent their final days, months and years in the dining commons listening to the astonishing tale that Posner wove, wondering which account to believe, his or 'Stijn's Story.'

There was one glaring similarity. Posner's version, like that of the artist-turned-illusionist, offered no fresh information about the Frick heist, who benefitted, and who didn't. The truth still lies buried with the artists, the thieves, the liars and their listeners/enablers.

Debts

Three experiences led to the creation of this story. The first occurred years ago when I saw *Bagdad Café* (*Out of Rosenheim* in Germany), a 1987 English-language, West German film directed by Percy Adlon. *Café* is a comedy-drama set in a remote truck stop and motel in the Mojave Desert. The film (highly recommended) is loosely based on Carson McCullers' novella *The Ballad of the Sad Café* (1951).

The second happened during a cross-country drive with my wife. Bored with the uninspiring topography of the Great Plains, she said, 'Tell me a story.' So, I tried. That origin story was far shorter than the one in these pages.

The third experience derived from time spent in a senior community in Mesa, Arizona.

I return to my wife. My debt to her goes beyond her plea for a story as we drove. Although she read and re-read the manuscript (I'm a sloppy writer), taking under consideration consistent character behavior, context, grammar and spelling, saying 'thank you' does not account for the depth of my gratitude. Any errors you find are on me.

My appreciation goes also to my art history teacher at Humboldt State, Julie Alderson. My wife Sheila, who was Julie's teacher, first aroused my curiosity about art history informally; several courses with Julie fleshed out the details.

Benjamin Rodefer, seasoned in the legitimate world of buying and selling art, schooled me on the plusses and minuses of fencing stolen art.

Finally, Wikipedia provided some specific information on subjects beyond my familiarity. Any inaccuracy in these pages is my responsibility.

Author

Stephen Carey Fox is a Navy veteran of the Vietnam Era and Emeritus Professor of History at Humboldt State University (Cal Poly Humboldt) where his teaching career spanned four decades.

Steve is the author of award-winning articles and book-length oral histories (with documentation) about the relocation and internment of Europeans of enemy nationality in the United States during World War II.

In retirement, he turned to writing fiction for the pleasure of 'telling lies for fun.' His books consider crime, history, feminism, reminiscence, family and contemporary political, economic and social issues.

Steve writes from behind northern California's 'Redwood Curtain' in Willow Creek, a village renowned as the home of Sasquatch (a.k.a. Bigfoot) and ‘medicinal gardens.’

Made in the USA
Columbia, SC
12 August 2024

39827349R00143